了解中國
用英文

楊天慶，楊磊 編著

五千年歷史精華，
美食美酒、奇葩典故，外國人怎麼能不懂！

東西方大不同，如何向外國人介紹那些華人特色文化？

家庭中的性別地位，中國是否已實現了兩性平等？
五和八是 lucky number、四諧音死，中文有哪些有趣的數字梗？
中華美食百百種，佛跳牆、過橋米線、宮保雞丁……一一為您端上！

目　錄

9. 中國的計劃生育政策是怎樣的？ What is Family Planning Policy in China?

10. 中國重視用法律手段保護婦女嗎？ Does China attach great importance to legally protecting women?

11. 如今，中國的丈夫和妻子是平等的配偶嗎？ Are husbands and wives now joint partners in marriage?

12. 關於老年人有哪些廣為流傳的格言？ What are the popular Chinese sayings about old people?

13. 你知道古代中國的退休制度嗎？ Do you have any idea about ancient China's retirement system?

14. 在中國老人願意說出自己的年齡嗎？ Do the elderly people in China like to disclose their age?

15. 中國目前採用什麼規章制度來照顧老年人？ What regulations have been adopted to take care of elderly people?

16. 社區是怎樣照顧老年人的？ What does a community do for elderly people?

17. 父母上了年紀後，兒女們會做些什麼？ What do children do when their parents get old?

文化與教育拾萃 A Glimpse of Culture and Education in China

1. 中國的名字有文化含義嗎？ Do Chinese given names have cultural connotations?

2. 什麼是風水？ What is Fengshui?

3. 黃曆上有哪些內容？ What is said on the yellow calendar?

4. 什麼是生辰八字？ What is the Eight Characters of a Horoscope?

5. 哪些數字是幸運數字？ What numbers are lucky numbers?

the college entrance examinations in China?

21. 你知道中國高校的學生宿舍情況嗎？ What are the dormitories like in Chinese universities and colleges?

22. 中國大學生的社會關係的基本格局是怎樣的？ What is the basic pattern of social relationships among Chinese college students?

23. 學生為何又稱「桃李」？ Why are students also referred to as "peach and plum" in Chinese?

24. 名落孫山是什麼意思？ What does mingluo Sun Shan mean?

飲食典故與趣談 Interesting Stories About Chinese Food

1. 八寶豆腐 Eight Treasure Tofu

2. 臭豆腐 Smelly Tofu

3. 麻婆豆腐 Braised Mapo Tofu

4. 魚香肉絲 Fish-Flavored Shredded Pork

5. 泡菜魚火鍋 Fish Hotpot with Pickled Vegetables

6. 東坡肉 Dongpo Meat

7. 東坡肘子 Dongpo Stewed Pork Shoulder

8. 宮保雞丁 Chicken Stir-Fried with Nuts and Chilli Pep-pers

9. 乾菜鴨子 Braised Duck with Dried Vegetables

10. 爆鱔卷 Stir-Fry Yellow Eel at High Temperature

11. 佛跳牆 Buddha Jumps over the Wall

12. 涮羊肉 Instant-Boiled Mutton

13. 閉門羹 Bimen Thick Soup

15. 臘八粥 Laba Rice Congee

15. 玉 米 粥 進 宮 How was Corn Porridge Introduced to the Imperial Palace?

16. 一品包子 Yipin Steamed Stuffed Buns

茶典故與趣談 Interesting Stories About Chinese Tea

酒典故與趣談 Interesting Stories About Chinese Alcoholic Beverages

前言 Preface

　　近年來，中國旅遊進一步蓬勃發展，英語導遊的素質也在不斷提高，但是外國遊客對英語導遊的期望值也越來越高。他們不僅希望英語導遊可以介紹中國美麗的風景和悠久的古蹟，也希望透過英語導遊更多地瞭解中國的文化和風土人情。英語導遊一般對中國文化都有一定程度的瞭解，但是外國友人的提問有時會是他們沒有特別留意的地方；或者有些內容他們也很熟悉，但是一時不知道怎麼用英語表達才好。為了提高英語導遊的綜合文化素養，催生策劃了本書，以滿足英語導遊的知識需求。

　　綜合看來，本書主要有以下特色：第一，作者權威。本書作者均具備豐富的英語導遊教學與實踐經驗，熟悉中國文化內容，瞭解英語導遊工作的實際需要。第二，選材豐富，內容實用。本書所選內容都是外國人感興趣的話題，涉及中國文化和導遊工作的方方面面，具有較強的知識性和趣味性。第三，語言地道、簡練。聘請外國專家審校，確保本書語言符合英語習慣，容易被外國遊客理解；另外本書盡量避免使用晦澀難懂的生詞和繁複的句式，而是選用常用詞和簡練的語句，使其口語化，適合講解。

　　本書既是英語導遊的好幫手，也是廣大英語愛好者不可多得的知識讀本。書中若有不足之處，敬請讀者批評指正。

旅遊幽默故事 Funny Stories

1 旅遊 Tourism

As travellers arrive in Hawaii, they learn at least two words: Aloha, meaning "Hello", and Mahalo, meaning "Thank you". One day a local resident was shocked when he heard a frequent traveller tell a newcomer that Mahalo was the Hawaiian word for "garbage". The resident asked where he learned that. He replied, "Well, it is written on all the garbage cans."

Notes: 1) Hawaiian 夏威夷人的 2) garbage 垃圾

A boastful man from a city visited a small town. One day, he took a taxi to tour the area.

"What is that building over there?" The visitor asked the taxi-driver.

"That is the town's pagoda, sir." replied the driver.

"Well, we can put up buildings like that in three weeks." said the visitor.

A little while later the visitor said, "And what's that building we're passing now?"

The driver replied, "That is an ancient palace built in the Qing Dynasty, sir."

"Is that so?" said the visitor, "I believe that people in the city where I live could put up a palace like that in two weeks."

A few minutes later they were passing a large monastery. The visitor again asked, "Hey, what's that building over there?"

"I am afraid I don't know, sir, " replied the taxi-driver. "It wasn't there this morning!"

Notes: 1) intentionally 故意地 2) monastery 僧院

During a trip to the island's remote beach, Mr.Zhang and his wife were talking to their local tour guide as they were lying on the sand. Mr.Zhang stated how unusual it was to have no television, newspaper or radio. "In fact," He continued, "it is going to be strange to return home and find out what's been going on in the real world."

No one spoke for a few moments. Then, without taking his eyes from the horizon, the guide replied, "I believed that's what you came here for."

Notes: 1) unusual 不平常的 2) horizon 地平線

Mr.Li thought he had found a way to convince his wife that she needed to take a trip to the mountains in order to relax herself. While Mr.Li was cooking, she agreed to watch his videotape introducing hiking techniques and showing the mountain's natural beauty.

Fifteen minutes later, she came into the kitchen and handed him the tape. "It was good," she said, "but I don't need it."

"But it's a 70-minute video," Mr.Li replied. "You couldn't have watched the whole thing."

"Yes, I did," she assured her husband. "I put it on fast-forward."

Notes: 1) convince 使確信 2) hike 徒步旅行 3) technique 技術

One day Mrs.Huang's daughter phoned her, saying that she and her roommates were going on a long-distance trip with two college men. Mrs.Huang asked if she'd considered how her father would react.

"Oh, Mom," the daughter said, "Tell him not to worry. We don't even know

these guys."

Notes: 1) long-distance 長途的 2) react 反應

Their tourism class went on a three-day field trip to the hilly countryside. At a large cavern, they followed a local tour guide into its deepest section. When he turned off the lights, all the classmates were overwhelmed by total darkness.

"Wow!" said a classmate. "I wish I'd brought my camera!"

Notes: 1) overwhelm 使不知所措 2) camera 照相機

A group of tourists decided to spend the afternoon at the beach. When they arrived there, one of them wanted to find a place to put on his swimming suit. When he found no changing facilities, he quickly got inside a car to put on his suit. Then he noticed a woman on the beach looking at him intently. She continued to stare as he struggled into his suit. The man was irritated because he thought that his privacy had been invaded. He approached the woman and asked, "Do you always watch people while they're changing clothes?"

"Do you always change clothes in other people's cars?" She retorted.

Notes: 1) facility 設施 2) intently（目光等）固定不動 3) irritate 激怒 4) privacy 隱私 5) approach 走近 6) retort 反駁

Mr.Li and his wife traveled in Southern Spain. After arriving, they ventured off to test their language skills. Right before dark, they pulled up to a small hotel, and Mr.Li got out to ask for a room for the night. A few minutes later, he returned with a strange look on his face and a small package in his hands.

"Did they give us a room?" his wife asked.

"I'm not sure," he replied, "but I did get this ham-and-cheese sandwich."

Notes: 1) package 包裹 2) cheese 乳酪

Mrs.Li's husband had packed his bag for a business trip. However, that

afternoon he received a call saying that the meeting had been cancelled. On the spur of the moment, Mrs.Li and her husband decided to spend a romantic, childfree weekend trip out of the city.

Mrs.Li quickly repacked her husband's suitcase, replacing his belongings with two wine glasses, candlesticks and candles. Then she dashed out to buy a bottle of wine. When she returned, the bag was gone. A note on the kitchen table read, "Sorry, love, the business trip is on after all. I'll call you when I get there."

Notes: 1) romantic 浪漫的　2) suitcase 手提箱　3) belongings 行李　4) candlestick 燭臺

A group of tourists hiked up a mountain to go deer hunting. They separated into pairs for the day. That night, one hunter returned alone, staggering under a big deer. "Where is your partner?" the other tourists asked.

"He fainted a couple miles up the trail." the man answered.

"You left him lying there alone and carried the deer back?"

"Yes," said the man. "I figure no one is going to steal my partner."

Notes: 1) stagger 蹣跚而行　2) partner 夥伴

It was late at night when Mr.Tan picked up his friends at the airport. Since it was their first visit to this area, Mr.Tan tried to describe the scenery they were missing as he drove home. When they rounded a bend, Mr.Tan commented, "From here, in the daylight, you can see a snow covered mountain beyond the blue lake."

One friend peered into the darkness and explained, "Oh, how theoretically beautiful!"

Notes: 1) scenery 風景　2) peer 凝視　3) theoretically 理論上

The owner of a small travel agency saw an attractive couple gazing at his travel posters. Suddenly inspired, he ran up and told them his idea. "I'll give you a free vacation in exchange for appearing in an advertisement endorsing our agency's vacations." They agreed with the agency owner.

Three weeks later, the agency owner met them at the airport, and they were back from the vacation. While the man checked on their luggage, the agency owner asked the woman about the trip. "The food on the travel was wonderful, " she said, "and the flight was a thrill. But I do have one question. Who was that man I had to sleep with every night?"

Notes: 1) gaze at 凝視 2) vacation 休假 3) in exchange for 作為……的交換 4) advertisement 廣告 5) luggage 行李

Next to the parking lot was the meadow where a local farmer grazed his cows. One day some tourists opened the door of their car to give their dog a breath of fresh air.After seeing the cows, the dog immediately began chasing them. Then the dog hit the electric fence, howling into woods. After an hour of hot pursuit, the owner stuffed the dog into the car again and then angrily demanded to know why the farmer hadn't put a warning sign on the fence. The farmer replied, "Well, I would have put one up, if I'd known your dog could read."

Notes: 1) graze 用牧草餵；放牧 2) howling 嚎叫 3) pursuit 追蹤

A tourist visited a zoo.As soon as she arrived at the monkey area, she immediately rushed up to a zoo attendant. "You should see what's going on in the monkey cage!" she exclaimed. "Four monkeys are sitting at table playing cards."

"So what?" answered the attendant, shrugging his shoulder. "They're only playing for peanuts."

Notes: 1) immediately 馬上 2) attendant 侍者；服務員 3) shrug 聳（肩）

At the wildlife park, visitors are frequently warned not to get too close to park animals because serious injuries could result from an attack by the large animals.

One day when Mr.Yang was in the tour group touring this park, he overheard a

tour guide tell the group about safety in the park.

"Now let's review what you should do when a large animal attack looks imminent. The first thing to do is to form a circle, standing as close together as you can. Make sure you're shoulder-to-shoulder with people next to you, keeping your back toward the center of the circle."

The tourists paid close attention to his every word as he continued, "Most of all--the final part is very important--always make sure that I am in the center of the circle no matter what happens."

Notes: 1) overhear 無意中聽到　2) imminent 即將發生的　3) shoulder-to-shoulder 肩並肩的

It had been a hot and tiring tour in this area, and the general store in the small town sold cool drinks. When Steven came out of the store, a light rain began to fall. As he stood outside, enjoying the rain's refreshing coolness, he noticed that several local people sitting in the store were giving him a nasty look. Steven asked if there was something wrong.

"Sir," one man said, "We would appreciate it if you'd come up here in the store. It's been six months since it last rained, and we want to make sure that all of the rain hits the ground."

Notes: 1) displeasure 不滿　2) appreciate 感激；欣賞

One weekend Zhang's family traveled through a remote and rather uninteresting section in the countryside. They stopped at a visitors' station, hopeful for a change of scenery. Their teenage son said to the young tour guide at the station, "What will we see on the scenic route that we haven't seen already?"

"What have you seen so far?" asked the tour guide.

"Nothing!" their son replied.

The tour guide answered, "Then you've seen most of it already."

Notes: 1) uninteresting 無趣味的 2) teenage 十幾歲的

A husband and his wife stayed for a year in a foreign country. In the first few weeks they were busy with adjusting to the new customs and culture. They were amazed at the friendliness of the local children. Whenever they drove through towns, the children would be standing on the side of the road, waving at them. The husband and his wife would give them a big smile and wave back.

Weeks later, the wife learned that in the local towns children will wave their hands to stop traffic so they can cross the street.

Notes: 1) adjust to 調節；改變以適應 2) wave 對……揮（手、旗等）

A tourist held up her camera to take pictures of native children at play when she was on an African jungle expedition. Suddenly the children began to yell in protest.

The tourist apologized to the tribe chief for her insensitivity and told him that she had forgotten that certain tribes believed a person lost his soul if his picture was taken. She kept explaining for her behavior, and the chief tried many times to get a word in, but to no avail.

Finally the tourist finished the long speech for her apology and allowed the chief to speak. The chief smiled and said, "The children were trying to tell you that you forgot to take off the lens caps."

Notes: 1) jungle 叢林 2) expedition 旅行；遠征 3) insensitivity 對別人的感受不敏感 4) behavior 行為

At the end of their one-week tour of scenic places along the mountain range, the tourists all picked up several common fossilized remains as souvenirs. But at the airport, customs agents asked one of the tourists to open his bag that contained the fossils. The customs agents detained all of them for about 30 minutes, and they

shook their heads and spoke to one another in their own language. Finally, one customs agent looked straight at the tourists. In halting English, he asked, "Are these new or old fossils?"

Notes: 1) fossilize 使成化石 2) detain 拘留 3) halting 躊躇的 4) fossil 化石

2 旅店 In Hotels

While visiting Thailand, Mr.Zhang and his wife decided to do some shopping. Not far from the hotel was a store with various items of clothing hanging up. On the store entrance door a sign indicated that the store was offering a 50% discount. When they entered the shop, a woman asked if she could help them. They said that they would like to look around on their own. She looked at them rather strangely.

Not finding anything suitable, Mr.Zhang and his wife thanked the woman and left. Suddenly, Mr.Zhang started to laugh and pointed to a small sign in English. It said, "DRY CLEANING SHOP."

Notes: 1) hang up 把……掛起來 2) reduction 減少 3) dry cleaning 乾洗

At the reception desk of a hotel, a couple asked for a room with a double bed. The clerk apologized and said that only twin bed rooms were available. The man was disappointed.He said, "My wife and I have been sharing the same bed for 44 years."

"Could you possibly put them close together?" The wife asked.

Several people nearby smiled and some commented, "How romantic."

The woman continued, "Because if he snores, I want to be able to punch him."

Notes: 1) double bed 雙人床 2) twin beds 兩張單人床 3)punch 用拳猛擊

On a business trip to a city to attend an international conference, a professor arrived at the city airport. He took a taxi to his hotel where he was greeted by his hospitable conference host. The cab driver requested 60 yuan for the fare, which seemed reasonable, so the professor handed him the money.

But the host grabbed the bills and called the cab driver a disgrace to the city for trying to overcharge visitors. The host threw half the amount at the driver and told him never to return.

As the taxi sped off, the host gave the remaining bills to the professor and asked him how his trip had been. "Fine," the professor replied, "but did you have to chase the cab away with my luggage in the trunk?"

Notes: 1) fare 車費 2)grab 抓取 3)disgrace 恥辱 4)trunk 後備箱

Mr.Zhang's daughter was a college student who joined a tour group and traveled in a city. Mr.Zhang called her every night at 10 to make sure she was all right since his daughter returned to her room at that time.

One Saturday, at about 10: 00, he called her room and was relieved when she picked up the phone. "Oh, honey," he said, "I'm so glad you're back in your room.Have a good rest."

"Dad," replied his daughter, "I'm just getting ready to go out!"

Notes: relieved 寬慰的

There is a hotel near the city.Its official maxim was "Give the customer what they want." The hotel staff's ability to meet that goal was tested one day when a large tour group overwhelmed the registration area.

One impatient man bullied his way through the crowd, banged his fist on the front desk and demanded, "I want a room that faces the ocean!"

The young clerk answered, "Certainly, sir.Atlantic or Pacific?"

Notes: 1) maxim 座右銘 2) bang 猛擊 3)Atlantic 大西洋 4) Pacific 太平洋

Staff trainees are required to perform many duties when undergoing basic training at a five-star hotel. One of these duties is to rake up leaves around the yard. The hotel training program teacher always screams that he wants every leaf swept into a pile.

Once, he found a lone leaf that his trainees had missed. He pointed to the leaf and roared, "What is this right here, trainees?"

One of the trainees looked straight at the teacher and replied, "A one-leaf pile, sir."

Notes: 1) rake up 耙集 2) a pile of 一堆 3) trainee 實習生

When a family travels with their cat, they usually stay at hotels permitting guests to bring along pets. However, on one late night on a recent road trip, they found themselves at a hotel that forbade animals. They successfully sneaked their cat past the front desk.

The next morning when the husband put the cat in a cardboard box and closed the flaps, this animal began to meow. On a crowed elevator, the husband coughed loudly to cover the sound of the cat. Everyone politely ignored the meows coming from the box.

When the elevator doors opened before the busy front desk, the husband bravely marched out, praying that the cat would shut up. Fortunately all the followers marched with him, coughing loudly all the way through the lobby and out the entrance door.

Notes: 1) sneak 偷偷地走 2) cardboard 硬紙板 3) flap 垂下物;（袋）蓋 4) meow 發喵喵聲;貓叫聲

Sam stayed at a hotel while attending a conference. Since he wasn't used to the big city, he was overly concerned about security. On the first night he placed a chair against the door and stacked his baggage on it. Then he put the trashcan on the top. If anyone tried to break in, he would be sure to hear him.

Around 1 a.m. there was a knock on the door. "Who is it?" my friend asked nervously.

"Dear guest," a woman on the other side yelled, "you left your key in the door."

Notes: 1) security 安全感 2) stack 堆積 3) trashcan 垃圾桶

Once, when a musician travelled across the country with her erhu, a two-stringed bowed Chinese instrument with a low register, she made a deal with a hotel owner. In exchange for a night's lodging, she would sing and play her erhu in the lounge for one hour and a half.

One night when it was time to perform, she was discouraged to see just one man sitting in front of the stage. She decided to perform. She felt pleased that she had entertained at least one person that evening. One hour and a half later after her performance, the musician stepped down from the stage when that man asked her quietly, "Can I go up to the stage to clean the floor?"

Notes: 1) lodging 借宿 2) lounge 休息室 3) entertain 娛樂

As head of housekeeping at a hotel, Ms.Yang tried her best to make sure the guests' rooms were spotless. But one day one guest stopped by her office that was always a mess.

"Oh, my!" she exclaimed.She seemed taken aback by the mess in the office. "What a mess it is! Is it your research lab?"

Notes: 1) housekeeping 客房部 2) mess 凌亂的狀態 3) research lab 研究實驗室

One day as a gentleman got into the hotel elevator, an elderly woman joined

him. She seemed friendly and made a few chatty remarks as they started upward. "I'm 92." she told the man.

"I can hardly believe it!" he exclaimed in congratulations. However, she gave him a look of surprise and replied, "I'm in Room 92."

Notes: 1) elevator 電梯 2) congratulations 恭喜

A Japanese man was travelling alone in France. He went to a tourist agency and asked the agent if she could help him find an inexpensive single room. Speaking in rapid French, the agent called a hotel. After a while, she put the phone down and said to the young man, "They have a room in your price range, but it is rather small."

"How small is it?" he asked.

Again the agent spoke into the phone in French. Then she turned to the man and said, "How tall are you?"

Notes: 1) reservation 預訂 2) inexpensive 價錢低廉的

One day a man called a hotel near the ocean to make reservations for a weekend stay.He was shocked when the inn clerk told him how expensive the room would be.

"Hold on a minute," he said. "I need to talk to my wife about the price of your rooms."

After relaying the price to his wife, the man added, "And that expensive room includes an ocean view."

"Good!" his wife gasped. "Ask the clerk if she will discount the price if we don't look out of the window."

Notes: 1) relay 重述 2) gasp 氣吁吁地説

During a trip to a non-English speaking country, a man and his friend stayed in an inexpensive guesthouse. After an exhausting tour, they returned to their lodgings, and they were all tired and thirsty. So they asked at the front desk in English to have two Seven-Ups sent to their room.

The drinks never came, so they went to bed.Early the next morning while they were still sleeping, the desk clerk phoned to them: "Morning call, seven up!"

Notes: 1) exhausting 讓人精疲力竭的 2) 7 Up 七喜

Susan saw a hotel offering numerous discounts to members of various groups, so she decided to have a try at the hotel for the night. She inquired the front desk clerk about the discounts. The clerk immediately read out a list of discounted items, but none of those applied to Susan.Susan joked by saying, "But I am left-handed."

"That will do," the clerk said, "Sign here."

Notes: 1) apply to 適用於 2) left-handed 慣用左手的

A man walked into a first-class hotel. He asked if there were any rooms available.

"What kind of room would you like?" the desk clerk asked politely.

The man picked up a pen to register and asked, "What have you got for around 60 yuan?"

The clerk replied, "Sir, the pen you're holding cost around 60 yuan."

A man came from a very remote area where there is still no electricity. For the first time in his life he left his village and went to visit a city where he stayed in a guesthouse. When he returned, his friends asked him how he had enjoyed himself.

"Well, the trouble was I couldn't sleep in the guesthouse." he told them.

"Why was that then?"

"The light was on in my bedroom all the time."

15

"Why didn't you blow it out, then?"

"I tried to, but it was inside a little glass bottle."

Notes: 1) electricity 電　2) blow out 吹熄（燈火）等

Tom stayed on the fifth floor in a hotel with his father. He came thundering down the stairs.

"Tom," his father called, "how many more times have I got to tell you to come down those stairs quietly! Now, go back upstairs and come down like a civilized human being."

Tom went upstairs as his father said.Several minutes later, he was back on the first floor and his father heard no noise.

"That's better," said his father. "Will you always come down the stairs like that in future?"

"That suits me," said Tom. "I slid down the banister."

Notes: 1) thunder 轟隆地響　2) banister 欄杆

The train was approaching to a city. A tourist said to his tour guide, "Do you often visit this city?"

"Yes," said the guide, "I tour the city with tour groups several times every year."

"Could you tell me which hotel offers the best service in the city?"

"The one located close to the city's center."

"Do you always stay there?" the tourist asked again.

"No, I've stayed in all the hotels here except that one close to the city center."

3 進餐 In Restaurants

A man stood up in a crowded restaurant and shouted, "Anybody lost a roll of five pound notes with a rubber band around them?"

There was a rush of people claiming to be the loser. The first to arrive was an old man.

"Here you are," said the man. "I have found your rubber band!"

Notes: 1) roll 卷 2) band 橡皮圈 3) claim 聲稱

A family was eating in a restaurant, which is close to a clinic.

"Dad," the son rushed to his dad and said, "is it true that an apple a day keeps the doctor away?"

"That's what they say." said his dad.

"Well, give me an apple right now, as I've just broken the doctor's window!"

Notes: clinic 診所

An inn owner locked up his place at 2 a.m. and went home to sleep. He had been in bed only a few minutes when the phone rang. "What time do you open up your inn in the morning?" he heard an obviously drunk man inquire.

The owner was absolutely furious. He slammed down the receiver and went back to bed. A few minutes later the phone rang again, and he heard the same voice ask the same question. "Listen," the owner shouted, "there's no sense in asking me what time I open my inn because I wouldn't let a person in your condition in..."

"I don't want to get in," the caller interrupted. "I want to get out."

Notes: 1) obviously 明顯地 2) furious 狂怒的 3) slam 猛地關上 4)interrupt 打斷

A man and his wife decided to eat out one night, but they failed to make a reservation. When they arrived at their favourite restaurant, they learned that several people had signed up for a table ahead of them. The man left their names with the hostess, and they sat in the reception area.

Soon afterwards an unhappy couple left the restaurant, complaining that the wait was too long. Within minutes, the hostess called, "Zhang Mei and Zhang Ming?" No one responded. She called again, but to no avail.

Quickly, the man convinced his wife that if they told the hostess that they were the Zhangs, they would get seated faster. As they approached her, she said, "Are you Zhangs?" the man nodded. "We've been expecting you," she informed them. "Your family is waiting for you in the dinning hall."

Notes: 1) hostess（餐廳）女招待　2) complain 抱怨

After a meal in a restaurant, a customer said to the restaurant's owner, "I am sorry that I can't pay you for this dinner because I have left my purse at home."

"It doesn't matter," the boss replied. "Pay me next time when you come for another dinner. However, you have to write down your name on the wall close to the entrance."

The customer said, "It is no good. Other customers will catch sight of my name."

"Why not take off your overcoat and hang it on the wall to cover your name?" said the boss.

At a restaurant, a party of diners was exhausting the waiter with their relentless demands. Through it all, the waiter remained patient and professional.

Finally one of the diners asked the waiter to take a photo for the group. He did it--from the neck down.

Notes: 1) relentless 持續不斷的 2) professional 職業的

When a man introduced his brother Wes to the owner of his favourite Chinese restaurant, the owner greeted him enthusiastically, saying, "Welcome, West." Wes shook his hand and smile, even though his name had been mispronounced.

All through the meal, the owner checked to make sure "West" was well served. Finally, Wes corrected him. "It's Wes, not West."

"Wes, not West?" asked the confused owner.

"Yes," Wes said. "Wes, no't."

"Ah," said the owner, and then he walked away with the teapot from Wes.

Notes: 1) enthusiastically 熱心地 2) teapot 茶壺

A man went to a coffee shop for breakfast. The waitress served him coffee and bread but no spoon.

"Hey," the fellow called to the waitress, "This coffee is too hot to stir with my finger."

A short time later, the waitress returned with another cup of coffee. "Here," she said. "This one is not as hot."

Notes: spoon 湯匙

The truck driver stopped at a roadside restaurant. The waitress brought him a hamburger, a cup of coffee and a piece of pie.

As the trucker driver was about to eat, three men in leather jackets pulled up on motorcycles and came inside. One grabbed the man's hamburger, the second one drank his coffee and the third one took his pie. The truck driver didn't say a word. He got up, put on his jacket, paid the cashier and left.

One of the motorcycle men said to the cashier, "He is not much of a man, is he?"

"He is not much of a driver, either," she replied. "He just ran his truck over the motorcycles."

Notes: 1) pull up 把車開到某處停下 2) grab 搶奪 3) cashier 出納

A couple was invited to eat at a new buffet restaurant. After they got their meals, the owner came over and asked, "How's everything?"

"Fine," replied the husband. "I enjoy buffets. I usually eat until my ankles hurt."

"Your ankles hurt?" asked the owner.

"Yes," said the husband. "My wife kicks me under the table when I've had enough."

Notes: 1) buffet 自助餐 2) ankle 踝關節

A man sat alone at an adjoining table in a restaurant. The waitress approached him and asked, "Are you waiting to be joined by a tall, thin woman with long hair?"

He answered, "In the larger scheme of my life, yes. But today I'm meeting my wife."

Mr.Li often took his seven-year-old son to the theatre to watch local plays. One evening before a performance, they ate at a nearby restaurant.He urged his son to eat his dinner. "Come on, my son," Mr.Li coaxed. "This casserole is as creative as one of the local plays."

His son took two bites and frowned. "Dad," he said, "is this dish a tragedy or a comedy?"

Notes: 1) coax 哄誘 2) casserole 沙鍋 3) creative 有創意的 4) tragedy 悲劇
5) comedy 喜劇

A man went to a restaurant for lunch and asked for the non-smoking section. A few minutes later, a waiter led him to the table and said, "This is the border line between non-smoking and smoking. Please do not breathe to your left."

At a restaurant in the centre of the city, a movie star handed the servant 50 yuan and told him to be cautious when parking her expensive car.

"I'll be careful with your car, ma'am," said the servant. "I have one car at home just like it."

Notes: cautious 十分小心的

As a man and his wife entered a crowded restaurant, the man requested a booth. The waitress glanced at the dinning hall, turned back to them and said, "I'm sorry, sir. I can't give you a booth, but I can give you a table with a view of a booth."

Notes: booth（餐廳等的）包間；雅座

Tom took Mary out to a fancy restaurant. They each had lobster, wine and a large dessert. As they sipped the wine, Tom said, "If my doctor saw me, she would be rather upset."

"Why?" asked Mary. "Does she have you on some kind of diet?"

"No, " said Tom. "I still owe her money."

Notes: 1) lobster 龍蝦 2) sip 抿了一口 3) diet 飲食;節食

A woman found a note on the sandwich menu offered in a restaurant: "We will pay you 20 yuan if you order a sandwich that we can't make." She ordered an elephant-ear sandwich.

Several minutes later, the waitress returned and said, "Here's your 20 yuan, ma'am. We can't make that sandwich."

"I'm not surprised, " answered the woman. "Where would you ever get elephant ears?"

"Oh, it's not the ears," said the waitress. "We're out of really big bread."

The manager of a restaurant said, "Our restaurant is very good. If you order an egg, you will get the freshest egg in the world.If you order hot coffee, you will have the hottest coffee in the world, and⋯."

"I believe what you said," said a customer. "I ordered a small steak just now. Is it the smallest steak in the world?"

Notes: steak 牛排

At a restaurant, a customer admired the colourful blouse of the waitress's uniform, "How can I get a shirt like that?" she asked.

"You have to work here if you want a blouse like mine," replied the waitress. "And I don't think that you want one that badly."

Notes: admire 羨慕

4 途中 En Route

A flight was experiencing considerable turbulence. One first-time tourist began praying. "Lord, " he said, "I'm a rich man. If you just let this plane land safely, I will give you half of everything I own."

The plane landed, and this man was the first one to get off the plane. A preacher caught up with him and tapped him on the shoulder. "Sir," he said, "I was on that plane with you. I also heard your prayer. Well, I am a preacher. On behalf of the Lord, I am here to collect what you promised to the Lord."

"I made the Lord a better offer," the rich man said. "I told him if he ever catches me on a plane again, he can have it all."

Notes: 1) turbulence 動盪；顛簸 2) preacher 傳道士 3) on behalf of 代表

A flight was rather dull, so when the pilot announced that they would be passing over the landscape area, a man thought he would have some fun. As a flight attendant passed by, he said, "I'd like a parachute, please. I'm getting off at the landscape area."

She nodded and walked away. A few minutes later she returned. "We're out of parachute," she told him apologetically, "but I checked around and there's a gentleman in the first-class with this really big umbrella..."

Notes: 1) pilot 駕駛員 2) parachute 降落傘 3) apologetically 道歉地

A motorist was driving along the motorway when, to his amazement, he was overtaken by a cyclist.

He increased his speed to 80 miles per hour, but once again the cyclist passed him.Eventually, the driver could stand it no longer and stopped.

"Thank heavens you've stopped," said the cyclist. "I have my braces caught in your back bumper."

Notes: 1) motorway 高速公路 2) amazement 驚奇 3) cyclist 騎自行車的人 4) brace（褲子的）背帶 5) bumper 保險槓

A sightseeing tour was aboard an open-sided bus.Because of heavy traffic, the drive couldn't make unnecessary stops. So, before each trip, he announced, "If your hat blows off during this ride, please raise your hand. I will then raise my hand. Everyone on the bus will raise a hand, and we will all wave good-bye to your hat."

It was rush hour, and a man was dashing to a train at the station. As he got close to the train, a plump and middle-age woman sprinted up from behind.She lost her footing on the smooth marble floor and slid onto her back close to the man's shoes. Before he could help her, however, she scrambled up. Gaining her composure, she winked at him, saying, "Do you always have beautiful women falling at your feet?"

Notes: 1) dash 猛衝 2) plump 豐滿的 3) sprint 衝刺 4) marble 大理石 5) scramble 匆匆忙忙 6) composure 鎮定；冷靜

A small car pulled alongside a limousine at a traffic light.

"Do you have a car phone?" the small car driver asked the guy in the limousine.

"Of course I do," replied the haughty deluxe-car driver.

"Well, do you have a fax machine?"

The driver in the limousine sighed. "I have that too."

"Then do you have a double bed in the back?" the small car driver continued.

Grey-faced, the other driver sped off. That afternoon he had a mechanic install a bed in his car.

A week later, the limousine driver passed the same small car, which was parked on the side of the road. Its back window fogged up and steam was pouring out. The limousine driver pulled up, got out of the car and banged on the back-window of the small car until the driver stuck his head out.

"I want you to know that I had a double bed installed inside my auto." the auto driver bragged.

The small car driver was unimpressed. "You got me out of the shower in my car just to tell me that!"

Notes: 1) limousine 大轎車 2) haughty 傲慢的 3) deluxe 豪華的 4) mechanic 機械工 5) unimpressed 沒留下深刻印象的

Miss Zhang is a deaf girl. When she first took an airplane flight by herself, her friend was worried because she had to change planes in another city. The airplane personnel assured them that they were accustomed to these situations and the deaf girl would be accompanied to her connecting flight. The deaf girl's friend was relieved.

The two had a cup of coffee, waiting in the airport lounge for an airport servant to accompany the deaf girl to Gate 6 for boarding. The deaf girl's friend was confident about the deaf girl's trip until she heard a voice on the loudspeaker announce, "Miss Zhang, please report to Gate 6 for boarding."

Notes: 1) companion 同伴 2) be accustomed to 習慣（於） 3) alleviate 減輕 4) loudspeaker 喇叭

On the third day of a motor trip, a couple's young son kept complaining about the heat, so they promised they would spend the night in a hotel with a swimming pool. At dusk, they pulled into a gas station and asked the attendant if he could direct them to the nearest hotel with a pool.

"Sure," he said. "Continue west on the main street, take a right at the first traffic light and then go about 300 miles.You can't miss it."

After the tour of a scenic place in the countryside, the tourists drove back home. They thought they knew the way. But after wandering the back roads for a while, they stopped to ask directions from a peasant sitting on his front porch. They asked if the road they were on was the right one. He answered with a "yes." Not being too convinced, they asked him if he was sure.

"It won't hurt to give it a try," the man replied. "You are lost anyway, aren't you?"

One day a car pulled up in front of a house. A woman hailed an old man, who was working outdoor. "Excuse me, how do I get to Main Street?"

"Well, go along this road to the end," he began. "Turn left two times and right two times. It's quartermile on the right."

She thanked him and drove away. About 20 minutes later, the same woman

pulled up again, calling, "Excuse me..." the same old man looked up. Surprisingly the woman recognized him, and her eyes became much widen. "Never mind, " she said, and she drove away immediately.

Notes: recognize 認出

As a teenage boy, he accompanied his mother on a long bus trip to visit a scenic spot. She was a young-looking woman at the time, even though she was 53 years old. On the return journey, the handsome driver stood outside the bus to assist them in boarding. "Help your sister with her bag." he suggested. As the boy turned to correct him, his mother nudged him and said sweetly, "Never mind, brother. You heard what the man said."

Notes: nudge 輕推

During the lunch hour, Lucy picked her friend up at her office to drive her to a relatively far away supermarket. Before dropping her off, Lucy had to stop at her office building to take care of a small matter. When they arrived, there were no free parking spaces, so Lucy quickly turned into the parking lot of the funeral crematory building where corpses were burned to ashes.

"You can't park here." her friend protested.

"Sure I can," Lucy replied. "You just sit here and cry while I run my errand."

Notes: 1) crematory 火葬場 2) corpse 屍體 3) protest 抗議；反對

When a man was driving a taxi in a city, he stopped to make a U-turn to pick up a customer on the other side of the street. But other cars prevented him from making the turn. Finally a woman stopped her car and motioned to him to go ahead.

As he passed her, the man opened his window and said, "Thank you." The woman lowered her window and replied, "Don't thank me. I don't trust you taxi-drivers."

Notes: motion 打手勢；示意

A mail truck broke down on a busy street. The truck driver pulled the vehicle onto the side of the street, put on the hazard lights and went to call a repair shop. Then he returned to the truck to wait.

A moment later, a car pulled up in front of the driver who thought that it was someone stopping to offer help. So he approached the car. A woman inside rolled down the window and said, "Will you mail this letter for me?"

Notes: 1) vehicle 車輛 2) approach 靠近

A high executive was speeding down a busy street, talking on his car phone. The police soon pulled him over. The executive completed his call and looked up at the office. "Yes?" he said.

"I bet you don't even know why I stopped you!" the police replied.

The executive said, "Yes, I know. You want to use my car phone."

Notes: executive 官員

A woman in the town called the police department and complained, "People are speeding on our street. Their speeding might endanger the lives of children who walk to school."

The next morning, she herself was stopped for speeding. "But, officer," she said, "I'm the person who called yesterday to tell the police about these speeders."

"Well then, madam," he replied, handing her a ticket, "you should be happy we caught one."

Notes: 1) endanger 使遭到危險 2) speeder 超速行車者

After a lady landed at the busy airport, she had difficulty in attracting the attention of any porters to help with her luggage. In desperation, she took out a 20-

yuan bill and waved it above the crowd.

In an instant, a young man was at her side. "Madam," said the man, "I'm an airport porter. You certainly have excellent communication skills."

Notes: 1) desperation 絕望 2) communication 交流

When this lady takes a taxi, she is generally shy about asking a taxi-driver to slow down. One day she took a taxi, and the driver went through his fourth red light and careened around a corner. She could keep silent no longer.

"Excuse me," she said quietly, "would you mind slowing down a little?"

The driver looked back at her, "What's matter?"

"I've been in three taxi accidents already," she yelled.

"That's nothing," he said proudly. "I've been in over a hundred."

Notes: 1) careen（車等）歪歪斜斜地疾駛 2) yell 叫喊

A tourist took a taxi for his excursion out of the city. On the way he patted the driver on the shoulder, asking some questions. His pat really horribly scared the driver.

"I am so sorry," the tourist apologized "I never expected to frighten you this way."

"It doesn't matter," answered the driver. "It is a misunderstanding. I have been driving the coffin van for years until last week when I began driving a taxi instead."

Notes: 1) excursion 短途旅行 2) horribly 可怕地 3) coffin 棺材

5 購物 Shopping

A lady worked in a very fine jewellery store. When she offered to help customers, they usually responded to her by saying, "No, thanks, I'm just looking."

One day a young woman was surveying an exquisite selection of golden rings.When the lady asked if she needed assistance, she said with a sigh, "No, thanks.I am just wishing."

Notes: 1) jewellery 珠寶 2) survey 審視 3) exquisite精美的

The woman was ahead of a man in a long line towards the cashier's. She was reading a paperback romance novel, and the man inched along behind her. When her turn finally came, she stepped aside, saying to the man, "You go ahead.I can't stop reading now. The man in the novel just carried her into his castle!"

Notes: 1) paperback 平裝本 2) inch 緩慢移動 3) castle 城堡

To help pass the time while waiting in line for the checkout at the supermarket, a mother quietly read a children storybook to her three-year-old son. The line moved slowly as her son became occupied in her reading stories.

By the time the mother finished the book, she found herself standing behind an elderly man who had allowed everyone in line to go ahead of him. When the clerk called for the next person, she asked the man if he was ready to go. "I was always ready," he said, smiling. "I just wanted to hear what happened to all the stories. It is very interesting."

One busy Saturday at the supermarket, a man pushed his loaded cart and arrived at a slow-moving line for checkout. The man asked the cashier, "How long will it be?"

"At least an hour and a half." relied the cashier.

To the cashier's surprise, he cheerfully stood in line and patiently browsed through the magazines. When his turn finally came, the cashier apologized for the waiting.

"Don't worry about it," he said. "I am in no hurry. My wife wants me to mow the lawn today."

Notes: 1) laden 裝滿的 2) browse 隨便翻閱 3) mow the lawn 修剪草坪

At the clothing store's counter, a woman handed the cashier her credit card. She waited for a long time while the cashier went away to verify the account. When she finally returned, the cashier said, "I'm sorry, this card is in your husband's name, and we can't accept it because the records show that he is deceased."

With that, the woman turned to her spouse, who was standing next to her, and asked, "Does this mean I don't have to prepare lunch for you today?"

Notes: 1) verify 證明 2) deceased 死去了的 3) spouse 配偶

A man was standing in a long checkout line at the department store.He would start grumbling because only one cash register was opened, but this time he decided to let it pass.

As the man waited, a young woman pulled up with an over-filled shopping cart. She looked exhausted. The man turned to her and said, "Another cash register really should be opened. If you feel uncomfortable about asking the store manager to open another register, I'll gladly ask the manager to do it."

"Oh, thank you, but no!" she exclaimed. "I am the mother of newborn twins and a two-year-old boy, and I don't want to go home in a hurry! Let my husband take care of all that a bit longer."

Notes: 1) grumble 發牢騷 2) register 收銀機 3) uncomfortable 不舒服的 4) twins 雙胞胎

Customer: "Last week when I was in your antique shop, I noticed a big mug with a flat head that holds a lot of beer. I'd like to buy it."

Dealer: "Sorry, ma'am, I can't do that."

Customer: "Why not?"

Dealer: "Because that is my brother-in-law."

Notes: 1) antique 古董 2) mug 大杯子

A man who had a hearing difficulty came into a store to buy an audiphone. A shop assistant said to him, "Our store sells a variety of hearing aids, and prices range from 10 yuan up to 200 yuan per audiphone."

"Could you give me all the details for the different audiphones?"

"Yes," said the assistant, "The audiphone that costs over hundred yuan has a sound automatic volume regulator. The 10 yuan hearing aid only consists of a conducting wire and an earphone, but its quality is excellent and the price reasonable."

"Does the 10 yuan aid work?" asked the man.

"Yes," replied the assistant. "So long as you clog up your ears with the earphone, other people can shout out at you."

Notes: 1) audiphone 助聽器 2) volume 音量 3) regulator 調節器 4) clog up 堵塞

An artist asked the gallery owner if anyone had shown interest in his paintings. "I've got good news and bad news," she said. "The good news is that a person inquired about your work and wondered if it would appreciate in value after you died. When I told him it would, he bought all 29 of your paintings."

"And the bad news?"

"The guy was your doctor."

One day a customer walked into a pet shop and told the clerk, "I need three small, gray mice and two dozen roaches."

The shop attendant was puzzled. She asked the reason for this strange request.

"Well," replied the man, "I'm moving out of the apartment that I have leased for a year. However, my lease agreement stipulates that I must leave the apartment both inside and outside in exactly the same condition I found them when I signed the lease agreement."

Notes: 1) lease 出租；租得 2) agreement 協定 3) stipulate 規定

A customer lit a cigarette and began smoking in the store where he just purchased a pack of cigarettes.

A store staff came over and said, "Sir, no smoking here, please."

The customer was completely confused.He responded, "Doesn't your store sell cigarettes? Why can't I smoke here?"

The store staff replied, "Our store also sells toilet paper."

Notes: 1) purchase 購買 2) a pack of 一包 3) toilet paper 衛生紙

The boss of a supermarket decided to make a surprise tour of the shops inside his supermarket. Walking through the warehouse, he noticed a young man lazily leaning against the wall. "How much are you being paid a week?" the boss asked him.

"A hundred dollars a week." answered the guy.

The boss pulled out his wallet and peeled off five 20 dollar bills. "Here's a week's pay," he shouted. "Now get out and don't come back."

Wordless, the young man stuffed the money into his pocket and took off. The warehouse manager stood nearby and stared in amazement.

"Tell me," the boss said. "How long has that guy worked for us?"

"He didn't work here," replied the manager. "He was just delivering a package."

Notes: 1) lazily 懶散地 2) amazement 驚奇 3) deliver 傳送

One day a lady was shopping with her nine-year-old son. She stopped at an automated teller machine to use her new ATM card. Worried about security, she told her son that she was going to get money out of the machine and to make sure no one was watching her. After the machine spit out five 20 dollar bills, her wide-eyed son said, "Do it again, Mom! Nobody's watching!"

Notes: 1) automated teller machine 自動存提款機 2)security 安全

A mother and her two little sons entered an ice-cream shop. The sons were eager to place their order for the newest kind of ice-cream.

"And you, mom, what would you like?" One son asked the mother.

"Nothing today," she replied. "I'm on a diet."

The other son was upset. He looked up at her. "Mom," he said, "does this mean you're going to help me eat mine again?"

An antiques collector was passing a small shop when he noticed a cat licking milk from a saucer. The man immediately realized the saucer was very old and valuable. He stepped into the shop with an uninterested look and asked to buy the cat.

"I'm sorry," the shop owner said, "but the cat is not for sale."

"Please," the collector urged, "I need a cat around my house to catch mice. I'll give you 20 yuan."

"The cat is yours," the owner said, taking the money from the collector.

"Listen," the collector said again, "I wonder if you could throw in that old saucer as well. The cat seems to like it."

"Sorry," the shop owner answered, "but that saucer brings me luck. Why, just this week I've sold 7 cats!"

Notes: 1) collector 收集者 2) lick 舔 3) saucer 茶碟 4) throw in 額外奉送

A young man worked at a 24-hour convenience store. One day a customer walked in and asked, "Is this store open all day, seven days a week, 365 days a year?"

"Yes." the young man answered, puzzled at the question.

"Well, then," he continued. "Why are there locks on the doors?"

Notes: 1) convenience 方便 2) be puzzled at 對……感到迷惑

A man went to a pet shop to buy a parrot.

"We have three parrots on sale," said the clerk. "This blue one speaks three languages and costs 120 yuan; the red parrot knows five languages and costs 220 yuan. The yellow one over there costs 500 yuan, but he doesn't talk at all."

"Five hundred yuan!" exclaimed the man. "How does it come so much?"

"Well," the clerk went on, "we don't know what he does, but the other two call him 'boss'."

Notes: parrot 鸚鵡

A sign appeared on the window of a clothing store in the center of a city. It said, "The store has been established for over 100 years. In the past years, we have pleased and upset customers; we have made money and lost money; we have been messed about, robbed and swindled. The only reason we stay in business is to see what happens next."

Notes: swindle 詐騙

One day a fellow was returning a duplicate globe to a store. As the clerk refunded him, she asked, "Why are you returning it?"

Displaying no emotional involvement, the guy said, "Wrong size.It's a small world."

Notes: 1) duplicate 複製的 2) refund 退款 3) emotional 感情上的 4) involvement 牽連

家庭關係 Family Relations in China

1 什麼是傳統的中國大家庭？ What is the traditional Chinese extended family?

We have all read storybook accounts of the traditional extended family with three or four generations living under one roof or cluster of roofs. The mutual support and interaction among family members that occurs in this setting has its enchanting aspects.

A traditional family was headed by the oldest male (grandfather or great-grandfather). Other members included the oldest male's younger brothers, sons and nephews, grandsons and grandnephews. Daughters were only a temporary part of the family. When a daughter married, she became a part of her husband's household. In this situation, it is not surprising that baby girls were often less than welcome. Male children, on the other hand, were necessary to carry on the family line. Eventually the oldest son carried the burden of responsibility for the extended family.

Even today, in the limited confines of a small apartment, there are remnants of the old extended family, but without the formal structure. One might say that today's extended family is more like a family collective, and some rural families are still likely to have three generations under one roof.

Notes: 1) storybook 故事書 2) extended family 大家庭 3) generation一代人 4) enchanting 迷人的 5) temporary 暫時的 6) confines 範圍 7) remnant 剩餘 8)

collective 集體

2 在傳統的大家庭中家長起什麼作用？ What was the family head's role in the traditional Chinese extended family?

A man carried a heavy burden of responsibility if he was the head of a household. He was almost solely responsible for the economic welfare of the family group and also imposed the discipline needed to ensure its good reputation. The latter tasks involved arranging socially advantageous marriages for his sons and daughters and living up to the high standards of the Confucian code for males. Of course, he took counsel with the other senior members of the extended family. In this system the father was the supreme ruler of the family, controlling its property, income, and members. He exerted power over his children and wife.

Notes: 1) welfare福利 2) discipline紀律 3) supreme 最高的

3 在這個制度裡婦女擔當的是什麼角色？ What was a woman's role in this system?

A woman had no legal status. She could not inherit property from her father or husband and had no money of her own. She was throughout her life subservient to and dependent upon men--first her father, then her husband, and finally her sons. A widow was usually not allowed to remarry.

A woman did achieve some status by giving birth to sons. She could even look forward to being able to play a dominant role when the brides of her sons were brought into household. If a family prospered, the wife could expect other wives and concubines to be added to the household, especially if she had failed to produce a son.

In ancient China it was normal and socially acceptable for a man to take more than one wife, especially if the first wife did not produce male offspring, provided that the family's income made it possible to support additional wives. Men of means were legally allowed to have as many concubines as they wanted. A number of emperors were notorious for the size of their harems. A concubine might be called by a variety of terms, usually involving the syllable qie（妾，concubine）. In modern Chinese, a wife is normally referred to as a taitai（太太）while a concubine is referred to as a "little taitai（小太太）". However there was always a distinction between the first wife and a secondary wife or concubine. The first wife was normally expected to have a superior position above later wives or concubines, and many may have welcomed their assistance as well as their company.

Notes: 1) inherit 繼承　2) subservient 充當下手的　3) dependent 依靠的　4) dominant 占優勢的　5) offspring 子孫；後代　6) harem 妻妾；女眷

4 在這個制度裡父親擔當的是什麼角色？ What was the father's role in this system?

The father in this system was the supreme ruler of the family, its property, income, and members. He exerted the power of life or death over his children and wife. However, most fathers, no doubt, were not too different from all human fathers and did not use their great power to mistreat their offspring. Most parents were undoubtedly just as concerned about the physical, moral, and social well-being of the children they had brought into existence as today's parents are.

Notes: 1) property 財產　2) existence 存在

5 孔子對此有什麼論述？ What did Confucius say about this system?

The traditional family was much influenced by Confucian philosophy. The Confucian ethic placed major emphasis on proper conduct in specific relationships. The generations established a hierarchy, which outlined the demands and privileges of each. Every member understood how he fit into that pattern.

In theory, this accorded with the Confucian principle of filial obedience-- children to parents, especially son to father. The theory is embodied in the "three bonds（三綱）" which established the relationship between the superior and the subordinate in the family and the state--the bond of loyalty on the part of subject to ruler; the bond of filial obedience on the part of son to father (children to parents); and the bond of chastity on the part of wives (but not of husbands).

Notes: 1) hierarchy 等級制度 2) filial obedience 孝順 3) embody體現

6 大家庭是怎樣分家的？ What is the Chinese family division?

When extended family members decide that their union has become, for economic or social reasons, impossible to sustain, they will agree to divide their family's resources and create financially separate new families. Generally this occurs after a senior generation has passed away and left two or more brothers. Although there is natural affection between the brothers, differences in their economic circumstances, as well as the number of their children, often lead to arguments that are most easily solved by family division. Traditionally the family will invite an experienced mediator as the third party to help with this separation.He/she will write an agreement that the brothers have to follow. After the division, each of the new units becomes financially independent. They live apart, even though they occupy the same courtyard. Although the family division is always considered an unfortunate event, the union of the extended family still remains intact, and the new units continue their cooperation and mutual support, on account of the memory of the old generation and cultural value placed on their family.

Notes: 1) economic 經濟上的 2) mediator 調解人 3) independent 獨立的 4) occupy 占用

7 什麼是「包辦婚姻」？ What is "arranged marriage"?

Traditional Chinese marriage was not the free union of two young adults to establish a new household. It was the movement of a woman from her birth family to her married family and assimilation into the new family. Traditionally friends and relations were constantly attentive for possible mates for young boys and girls. In spite of this, professional help was sometimes needed. Thus professional matchmakers（媒人）were a constant feature of the Chinese social scene.

Typically matchmakers representing the man's family would approach the woman's clan. Token presents and horoscopes were exchanged. If the offer was not wholly unacceptable, the girl's birth date would be written on red paper and given to the matchmaker, who would return to the man's family. The man's family would invite a professional fortune-teller to interpret the horoscopes. If the interpretation satisfied both families, the red cards with the family background of the pair would be exchanged. Presents were exchanged between the families and then another professional was paid to find an auspicious date for the wedding ceremony. Finally the groom, relatives and friends went to the girl's home and accompanied her to his home, where she would then become part of his family. According to older

traditions, the bride and groom didn't see each other until he lifted the veil from her face in the wedding chamber.

When the new marriage law was put in force with the establishment of the People's Republic, arranged marriages were officially prohibited. People realized that marriage should be based on the complete willingness of the two parties to become husband and wife. Neither party could use compulsion, and no third party was allowed to interfere. However, in some remote villages, young peasants still currently sometimes seek the help of matchmakers. But the young people have the freedom to accept or reject the proposed candidate.

Notes: 1) union 結合　2) assimilation 同化　3) attentive 注意的　4) matchmaker 媒人　5) horoscope 占星術　6) unacceptable 不可接受的　7) fortune-teller 占卜者　8) veil 面紗　9) willingness 自願；樂意　10) reject 拒絕　11) candidate 候選人

8 中國人在選擇結婚的年份和日子上有什麼講究嗎？

Are there any rules in choosing the year and the date to get married in China?

In China a traditional family carefully selects a following auspicious time for marriage. It is a belief that a good beginning is half done.

In the Chinese lunar calendar, the first "solar term（立春）" which occurs 45 days before the spring, symbolizes the beginning of the New Year. It is an auspicious year to hold a wedding ceremony when the first "solar term" occurs two times in the same lunar year, one in the beginning of the year, and the other at the end of the same year. It is called "double first solar terms（雙春）".

When one month is added to make the lunar calendar year correspond to the solar year, it will be 13 months in all. The 13th month is called runyue（intercalary month，閏月）. Run means "nourish or irrigate" signifying that love will nourish newly married couples who hold their wedding in this lunar year, and they will live together in harmony. When the "double first solar terms" and an intercalary month occur in the same lunar year, it will be a double auspicious year.

At present, once a bridegroom's family finalizes the wedding day, they will confirm the day with his bride's family. Some families may invite a fortuneteller to decide if the proposed wedding day is auspicious or they may consult the Huangdi Calendar（Almanac，黃曆）for reference. The calendar is a general ancient almanac providing information related to the dates of wedding, omens, lunar festivals and seasons, and basic knowledge of farming and planting.

Notes: 1) solar 太陽的 2) symbolize 象徵；標誌 3) correspond with 符合 4) intercalary 閏的 5) signify 表示……的意思 6) harmony 和睦；融洽 7) auspicious 吉利的 8) almanac 曆書 9) omen 兆頭

9 中國的計劃生育政策是怎樣的？ What is Family Planning Policy in China?

China's family planning policy was formulated in the early 1970s. The State Family Planning Commission sets the overall targets and policy direction. Family planning committees at the provincial and county levels devise local strategies for implementation. "One is enough" proclaimed posters that went up all over the land. It has been pushed forward as one of China's basic state policies and has contributed to its socioeconomic development. The basic requirements of family planning are late marriages and late childbearing, so that couples have fewer but healthier babies while adhering to the one child per couple policy.

A flexible family planning policy has been adopted for rural people and ethnic

minorities. In rural areas, couples may have a second baby in exceptional cases, but must wait several years after the birth of the first child.And each ethnic group may work out different regulations in accordance with its wishes, population, natural resources, economy, culture and customs.

Notes: 1) formulate 系統地闡述（或説明） 2) State Family Planning Commission 計劃生育委員會 3) overall 總的來説 4) target 目標 5) provincial 省的 6) strategy 策略 7) implementation 履行；執行 8) poster廣告（畫）；佈告 9) socioeconomic 社會經濟的 10) childbearing 生育 11) adhere to 擁護；支持 12) exceptional 例外的 13) ethnic 少數民族

10 中國重視用法律手段保護婦女嗎？ Does China attach great importance to legally protecting women?

China attaches great importance to providing legal protection for females. In 1950 the Central People's Government issued a marriage law, which already specified the rights and responsibilities of both husbands and wives. This provides us with a picture of today's new family.

The first constitution adopted in 1953 has an equal rights clause. It declares, "Women enjoy equal rights with men in all spheres of political, economic, cultural, social, and family life. Men and women enjoy equal pay for equal work. Men and women shall marry of their own will. The state protects marriage, the family, and the mother and child. The state advocates and encourages family planning."

In 1992 the Fifth Session of the Seventh National People's Congress approved the People's Republic of China Law on the Protection of the Rights and Interests of Women（《婦女權益保護法》）. This law further enhanced the social status of women and guaranteed their basic rights and interests.

Notes: 1) sphere 領域 2) session 會議；集會 3) National People's Congress 全國人民代表大會 4) guarantee 保證

11 如今，中國的丈夫和妻子是平等的配偶嗎？ Are husbands and wives now joint partners in marriage?

Husbands and wives both have the right to work, study, and take part in social and political activities. Both have the right to own, use, and dispose of commonly held property. Each has the right to inherit from the other.Both husband and wife are responsible for the care and support of any children they may have. Either husband or wife may sue for divorce, but the man may not seek a divorce while the wife is pregnant nor within one year after the birth of the child.

Generally divorce rates are low in China. Couples are encouraged to work out their problems with the help of their relatives, friends or neighbourhood residence committee staff, who do everything possible to keep couples from separating. If there is one percent chance of saving a marriage, they expend all their efforts to overcome the 99 percent of difficulty. Divorce will be granted if these efforts at mediation fail. Even in the case of divorce, both parents are responsible for the support of any children. Custody may be given to either parent, depending on which is more suitable under existing circumstances.

Notes: 1) dispose 處置 2) pregnant 懷孕 3) rate 比率 4) circumstance 環境；情勢

12 關於老年人有哪些廣為流傳的格言？ What are the popular Chinese sayings about old people?

In ancient China a man of 60 could carry a staff within his village. By the age

of 70, he could walk with the aid of the staff--a symbol of longevity--in the country, and by the age of 80, he could carry it before the Dragon Throne and did not have to kneel before the emperor. Anyone who reached the age of 90 was regarded as being sufficiently venerable for the emperor to heed his advice. A poetic line from the Tang Dynasty says, "A man of 70 is rarity from the ancient times（人生七十古來稀）".

Notes: 1) sufficiently 足夠地 2) venerable 可尊敬的 3) rarity 稀有

13 你知道古代中國的退休制度嗎？ Do you have any idea about ancient China's retirement system?

In ancient China, the retirement system only applied to government officials and officers. In Zhou Dynasty, officials were required to retire at the age of 70. In Han Dynasty, the retirement arrangement began to merge into the official bureaucratic system, and this continued until Ming Dynasty. Between the Ming and Qing dynasties, officials commonly retired at the age of 60.

Different dynasties provided different amounts of old-age pension. Several things determined how much of a pension retired officials would receive. These included the individual's age, official status, and contributions to the government. In the Han Dynasty pensions that amounted to 1/3 pre-retirement salary could be given to those whose annual salary was equivalent to 2,000 shi（石） of grain and above. Shi is a unit of dry measure for grain equal to 100 litres. During the Tang Dynasty the court government granted retired officials land that could be inherited down to the later generations.

Notes: 1) retirement 退休 2) merge 合併 3) bureaucratic 官僚政治的 4) contribution 貢獻 5) pension 養老金 6) be equivalent to 相當於

14 在中國老人願意説出自己的年齡嗎？ Do the elderly people in China like to disclose their age?

The elderly were--and still are--revered largely due to the deep experience in life and wisdom. By the time one has grey hair, one is expected to have acquired some wisdom and to have earned the right to respect. Some elderly people are quite happy to? reveal their age, especially if they feel they look young for their age. If the elderly people want to talk about their age, they themselves may easily bring up the topic and ask the other person to guess how old they are. They normally expect to be complimented on their youthfulness rather than being told that they look old!

Notes: 1) revere 尊敬 2) compliment 恭維；讚美

15 中國目前採用什麼規章制度來照顧老年人？ What regulations have been adopted to take care of elderly people?

Under the planned economy, all government functionaries, and urban and mine workers and staff enjoy medical care when sick or injured. In rural areas, co-operative medical services based on voluntary and mutual aid among the peasants are funded mainly by townships and villages, though each township member pays a small sum each year into the fund.

Since the 1990s China has actively promoted the reform of its old-age, unemployment and medical insurance systems. The State Council has promulgated Regulations on Unemployment Insurance（《失業保險條例》）, Interim Regulations on the Collection of Social Insurance Premium（《社會保險費徵繳暫行條例》）, and the Regulations on Guaranteeing Urban Residents' Minimum

Standard of Living（《城市居民最低生活保障條例》）. These regulations have integrated old age, unemployment, and medical insurance, which have provided legal guarantee for the implementation of the social security system. The coverage of basic old-age insurance has constantly expanded from state and collectively owned enterprises to enterprises of various types and institutions.

Notes: 1) functionary 公務員　2) co-operative 合作的　3) township 鎮　4) unemployment 失業　5) insurance保險　6) promulgate 頒布　7) interim 臨時的　8) premium 保險費　9) integrate 使成一體；使結合　10) enterprise 企業

16 社區是怎樣照顧老年人的？ What does a community do for elderly people?

China is encouraging communities to provide services for elderly people. Usually community services are set up in neighbourhoods where elderly people are organized to read, play cards, exercise, or practice painting and calligraphy. In addition, communities set up special teams to pay regular visits to the elderly at home, help them clean rooms and wash clothes, or accompany the elderly to do shopping in department stores or visit medical doctors in hospital. Elderly people in many cities enjoy preferential treatment, including free visits to parks, museums and cultural centres, and city bus transportation.

Notes: 1) neighbourhood 近鄰　2) calligraphy 書法　3) preferential 優先的；優惠的

17 父母上了年紀後，兒女們會做些什麼？ What do children do when their parents get old?

Traditional family ties remain strong. The concept of "four generations live under the same roof" continues to strongly influence most people in China, who still refuse to have their parents spend the remaining years of their lives in special homes for the elderly. Sons and daughters believe it is an honour and a privilege to have their parents living with them, even in the confines of a crowded city apartment or a small village house. Among married couples, many are currently still living with one of the spouses'parents who help look after grandchildren and do housework.

Many young Chinese couples have only one child. Those one-child families have established closer relations between children and parents. Children also realize that one day they will be responsible to look after their parents. More and more of the elderly people living in the cities prefer living by themselves. The best situation is to have parents and their adult children live in the same neighbourhood.Ideally, the parents' residence is no farther than a half an hour by bus from where their children live. Young people often hire nurses or housekeepers to take care of their parents while they are fully occupied with their work.

Children in rural areas financially support and look after their parents and grandparents. When the elderly are in good health, they continue to work in fields, and their adult children join in them during the period of a busy season. When the elderly cease working in the fields, their children begin to take their place. Children guarantee their basic needs and give them some pocket money for their daily expenses.

Notes: 1) spouse 配偶 2) reside 居住

文化與教育拾萃 A Glimpse of Culture and Education in China

1 中國的名字有文化含義嗎？ Do Chinese given names have cultural connotations?

There are a variety of Chinese given names（名字）usually made up of one or two characters. Chinese characters like fu（happiness，福），lu（fortune，祿）or shou（longevity，壽）sound auspicious. So traditionally one of them serves as a given name, which typically expresses the "happiness" that everyone desires.

The Five Elements（五行學）are the five basic natural substances.They are jin（metal，金）, mu（wood，木）, shui（water，水）, huo（fire，火）, and tu（earth，土）. Ancient Chinese philosophers believed that "Wood begets fire, fire begets earth, earth begets metal, metal begets water, and water, in its turn, nourishes wood." Some parents thus ask a fortuneteller to study their child's four-pillar-birth-chart. If the prediction states that there is a shortage of a certain substance like jin (metal), for example, in the child's life span, the parents will add a Chinese word that contains the radical of jin into the child's given name. The parents expect that their endeavour will make up for the shortage of that substance.

In addition, some given names are offered to commemorate the time or place of a child's birth.These include chunsheng（born in spring，春生）, husheng（born in Shanghai，滬生）and others. Some names may also reflect periods of history. Given names like guoqing（celebration of the founding of new China，國慶）or

jiefang（liberation，解放）would likely be offered to children who were born in 1950s.

Notes: 1）typically 作為特色地；典型地　2）beget 引起　3）prediction 預言 4）endeavour 努力 5）commemorate　紀念

2 什麼是風水？　What is Fengshui?

Ancient Chinese traditionally believed that the movements of the sun and moon affected spiritual currents that influenced people's daily lives. This "cosmic breath" is known as Fengshui（wind and water，風水）. It is said that it was also affected by the form and size of hills and mountains, the height and shape of buildings, and by the direction of roadways. Ancient people were aware of the importance of geomancy（divination by means of lines and figures）in the location and orientation of buildings and other structures.

Geomancy began during the Zhou Dynasty（1046 BC--256 BC）. A manual codifying of the rules of the art was published around 320. In addition to determining the orientation of buildings and doors, the Fengshui masters also countered the influence of negative cosmic breath by the use talismans (dragons and other symbols) on buildings and other structures and charms (power words and other inscriptions) on paper scrolls or tablets.

Notes: 1）affect 影響　2）cosmic 宇宙的　3）geomancy 抓沙撒地占卜　4）divination 占卜　5）orientation 方向；方位　6）manual 手冊　7）codify（系統地）編纂　8）negative 消極的 10）talisman 護身符

3 黃曆上有哪些內容？　What is said on the yellow calendar?

The yellow calendar adheres to the traditional view of good and bad days, detailing what should be done or avoided in detail on each day. The influence of these beliefs and customs varies among individual Chinese people. Some are more traditional in their beliefs and behaviour than others. These injunctions include the best and worst days for burying the dead, getting married, signing contracts, visiting friends, exchanging gifts, travelling and housecleaning.

Notes: 1) detail 細節；詳述 2) behaviour 行為 3) injunction 命令；指令 4) contract 契約；合約 5) housecleaning 清掃房屋

4 什麼是生辰八字？ What is the Eight Characters of a Horoscope?

The eight characters of a horoscope is a Chinese conceptual term in Chinese astrology. It describes the four components creating a person's destiny or fate. These four components are the year, month, day, and time (hour) when he/she was born. Since in Chinese, each of these components is expressed by two characters, which are a combination of the Heavenly Stems（天干）and Earthly Branches（地支）, yielding a total of eight characters. The Eight Characters are also known as the 4 Pillars of Destiny（四柱命）because these 4 pillars make up a chart or configuration of eight characters, which helps a fortuneteller determine a person's qualities, relationships, potential for a good career, and health risks.

In ancient China, when parents looked for a prospective wife or husband for their son or daughter, they had to consider a number of factors. One of the factors was to see if the prospective couple would be auspicious based on their four-pillar-birth-chart in conjunction with the Chinese Almanac（黃曆）. If the prediction did not feel right, the marriage would be called off.

Notes: 1) conceptual 概念上的 2) astrology 占星術 3) component 組成部分

4) destiny 命運 5) pillar 支柱 6) configuration 表面配置；形態 7) conjunction 連接

5 哪些數字是幸運數字？ What numbers are lucky numbers?

The number five is of significant importance in Chinese civilization. There are five elements of nature (metal, earth, fire, water, and wood), five tastes (salty, spicy, bitter, sweet and sour), five sacred mountains of Daoism, among other examples.

The number eight is also very important. It is significantly conspicuous in legends, myths and various practices.There are the fictional "Eight Immortals." who represent the eight conditions of life--poverty, wealth, aristocracy, peasantry, age, youth, masculinity, and femininity, as well as the Eight Diagrams, which form the basis for The Book of Changes. The number eight also rhymes with the Chinese word fa, which means getting rich.

Conversely the number four is a very unlucky number because in Chinese it sounds like the word for death.Thus Chinese try to avoid using the number four.

Notes: 1) conspicuous 顯眼的 2) peasantry 農民 3) masculinity 男子氣 4) femininity 陰柔 5) conversely 相反地

6 什麼是「印章」？ What is "name seal?"

People in China traditionally use Chinese name seal to stamp as personal signature. Many official documents have to be stamped with name or company seals. The use of name seals is one of the most conspicuous elements in Chinese business system and government offices. Chinese artists like to stamp their personal seals on their paintings rather than signing their names in the western way.

After paper was in use, people started to stamp the paper with an engraved seal. The surface of the seal that touches the paper is usually moistened with red ink paste.Earlier name seals were made of stone and were called fengyin (封印) or "stone seals". Seal materials now include jade, gold, brass, stone, wood, and the like. An experienced seal engraver is able to write Chinese scripts in different styles and arrange styled characters in a perfect balance.

Notes: 1) seal 印章 2) signature 簽名 3) engrave 雕刻 4) moisten 使……濕潤 5) ink paste 印泥 6) script字體

7 中國的禮儀中有哪些共有的行為規範？ What are the common rules of behaviour in Chinese etiquette?

During the early generations following the invention of eyeglasses in China, it was considered exceptionally rude for a person wearing eyeglasses to speak to someone without first removing their glasses.

The handshake is now a common form of greeting among most Chinese. The traditional greeting is to cup one's own hands (left over right), chest high, and raise them slightly while bowing. Young people in China currently tend to simply nod as a greeting. To some extent, this evolution reflects the ever-increasing pace of modern life.

It is polite to use both hands when offering an object such as a gift or a drink to someone as well as when receiving something from someone.

At hosted meals, it is the responsibility of the host--not waiters or servants--to see that the guests' drinking glasses are refilled.It is also mandatory in Chinese etiquette for the host to accompany each guest to the door when a meal or party ends.

Notes: 1) to some extent 從某種意義上講　2) ever-increasing 不斷增加的　3) mandatory 義務的；強制的

8 怎樣理解中國人的熱情好客？　What are the characteristics of Chinese hospitality?

The Chinese people remain a courteous and caring people. With their inherent kindness toward visitors, many Chinese are always offering to help foreign visitors in need. Sometimes it also appears to be a national custom for them to offer to share their food and other possessions with visiting foreigners when they are thrown together on trains and in other situations.

A banquet remains an important aspect of social occasions. Foreign visitors in China are often overwhelmed by a typical meal consisting of cold plates, hot dishes, soup and rice. They may consider this a lavish spread. However, it demonstrates the Chinese goodwill and hospitality that foreign visitors can readily appreciate.

Notes: 1) inherent 固有的　2) occasion 場合　3) lavish 慷慨的　4) readily 樂意地；欣然

9 中國的人際關係是怎樣的？　How do Chinese people get along with others?

China is generally a collective society.People emphasize relationship and group affiliation, whether to their family, school, or work unit.In order to maintain a sense of harmony, they will act with decorum at all times and will not do anything to make someone embarrassed. In most cases, they are willing to subordinate their own feelings for the good of the group. If someone disagrees with what another person says in public, the person may remain quiet. This is a way to give face to the other person.

Notes: 1) collective 集體的 2) relationship 關係；人際關係 3) affiliation 聯繫；從屬關係 4) decorum 端莊；得體 5) embarrassed 尷尬的

10 什麼是人情？ What is renqing?

Renqing literally means "human feelings or kindness" that enable a bilateral harmonious flow of personal or social transactions among family members or associates.Such human kindness includes parent's love toward children, filial piety for parents from children, happy interpersonal relations among brothers and sisters, and the like.

In social transactions, renqing works as a kind of tangible service or an abstract emotion.There is a popular old saying, "If you give me a drop of water, I will repay you with a bubbling spring（滴水之恩、湧泉相報）" The saying indicates that you should keep firmly in mind the favors other people have done for you and doubly repay a favour whenever an opportunity permits. Those who are aware of "giving" and "taking" are always regarded as people with conscience.

Notes: 1) bilateral 雙邊的 2) harmonious 和諧的 3) transaction 辦理、處置 4) associate 同伴 5) interpersonal 人與人之間的 6) tangible 有形的 7) abstract 抽象的 8) bubble 汩汩地流 9) doubly 加倍地 10) conscience 良心

11 中國人有午睡的習慣嗎？ Do Chinese people take daily noontime nap?

One Chinese custom still prevails in some areas and generally comes as a surprise to many foreigners who visit China for the first time.It is the noontime siesta, known as wuxiu（midday rest，午休）in Chinese.

In ancient agricultural civilization people got up with the sun, worked in the fields until midday, and then took a long break before going back to work and continuing until sundown.

In some places, the midday break during summer months lasts for up to three hours, beginning at noon or before. In winter it is usually two hours. However, in some business firms and factories, the length of wu xiu varies, and in some cases it has been eliminated altogether.

Notes: 1) siesta 午睡 2) agricultural 農業的 3) sundown 日落 4) vary 不同

12 中國古代的教育情況是怎樣的？ What do you know about education in ancient China?

The Chinese education system accompanied the birth of Chinese civilization. The Shangxiang（上庠）was a legendary school that taught young nobles in the Youyu（有虞）period in ancient China. Teachers at Shangxiang were generally erudite, elder and noble persons.This may be the origin of education in China.

In the Zhou Dynasty, the curriculum in school centred on the so-called "Six Arts": Rites, Music, Archery, Chariot-Riding, History, and Mathematics. At that time, numerous different schools enrolled students. One of the schools was Confucianism and one of Confucius's famous sayings declared, "Provide education for all people without discrimination（有教無類）." Another was "Teaching according to the student's ability（因材施教）."

Emperor Wudi（漢武帝）made Confucianism the orthodox philosophy of the Han Dynasty. Taixue（太學）was established to train civil servants for the empire. Taixue literally means "Greatest Learning" and it is the highest rank of educational establishment in Ancient China between Han Dynasty and Sui Dynasty. Gradually the curriculum focused on The Four Books and The Five Classics. Imperial examinations began in 605 AD. All those taking the examination were required to pass their local tests before the final examination in the capital. Private schooling（私塾）, where one teacher taught a small group of students from wealthy families, was the dominant mode of education. Feudal China's ancient educational system remained in place until 1905, when it was abolished and replaced by a more modern system.

Notes: 1）civilization 文明　2）erudite 博學的　3）mathematics 數學　4）discrimination 歧視 5）orthodox 正統的 6）curriculum 課程 7）abolish 廢除

13 古代考試授予哪些頭銜？ What degrees were granted in ancient examinations?

Below are a few types of degrees granted in ancient China:

1.Shengyuan（生員）, also called xiucai（秀才）, granted after passing the exams held at the county level each year.

2.Juren（舉人）, granted after passing the exams held at the provincial level every three years.

3.Jinshi（進士）, granted after passing the exams held in the capital every three years.

14 「老師」在中國文化裡有特殊的含義嗎？ What is the meaning of laoshi?

Laoshi, the Chinese words for a teacher at any level, is not merely a designation of social rank and function, but a term signifying considerable respect and deference. Perhaps the greatest difference between Chinese laoshi and American

professors is the quality of the relationships they tend to have with their students. In China, laoshi is expected to take a strong interest in the development of each student as a whole person. To a certain extent, the laoshi's role overlaps that of the student's parents. The role of a lao shi is jiaoshu yuren（教書育人）, which is literally translated as "to teach and to educate（nurture, bring up）people."

Notes: 1) designation 稱號　2) deference 聽從；尊重　3) overlap 重疊 4)bring up 養育

15 中國的義務教育情況是怎樣的？ What is the compulsory education like in China?

In 1986 the fourth session of the Sixth National People's Congress passed the Law of the People's Republic of China on Compulsory Education（《中華人民共和國義務教育法》）. It was revised during the 22nd session of the tenth NPC Standing Committee on June 29, 2006. This law stipulates that compulsory education must carry out the national policy of education, implement quality-oriented education, and improve the quality of teaching. The goal was to enable all school-age children to develop in a well-rounded way, including physically, intellectually, morally, and aesthetically. The law also stipulates that the departments in the national and local governments concerned with education should ensure the right of all school-age children to receive compulsory education. Children who are six years or older should be sent by their parents or legal guardians to school to study and complete the Nine-Year Compulsory Education program.

Compulsory education consists of two periods: primary education and junior secondary education. No tuition is collected for compulsory education. The state provides subsidies to poor families so their children can go to school.

Notes: 1) revise 修訂　2) implement 履行、實施　3) in a well-rounded way 全

面地　4）intellectually 智力上　5）morally 道德上　6）aesthetically 審美地　7）primary 初級的　8）secondary（教育、學校等）中等的　9）tuition 學費

16 中國的學前教育情況是怎樣的？ What is the preschool education like in China?

The Chinese government attaches great importance to preschool education. In cities and towns, educational departments, government organizations, enterprises, sub-district offices or individuals operate kindergartens or day-care centers. In rural areas, towns and villages sponsor kindergartens.

Kindergartens fall into three grades: The junior grade admits children at the age of three to four years old; the middle grade, four to five; and the senior, five to six. Nurseries take care of children under three. A variety of classes are offered, including elementary reading, writing, and arithmetic, as well as music, art and physical education.

Notes: 1) attach importance to 重視　2) preschool 學前的　3) kindergarten 幼兒園　4) nursery 托兒所　5) arithmetic 算術

17 中國的小學教育情況如何？ What is the primary education like in China?

The Chinese primary education system generally mandates that students study for six years, with some schools offering five years. According to the Nine-Year Compulsory Education Law, primary and junior middle schools are tuition-free and located so as to make it easy and convenient for students to attend school.

Children begin schooling when they are six to seven years old. They attend

primary schools in their neighbourhoods or villages. Parents pay a small fee per term for books and other expenses such as transportation, food, and heating.

The primary-school curriculum consists of Chinese, mathematics, physical education, music, drawing, and elementary instruction in nature, history, and geography, combined with practical work experiences around the school compound. A foreign language is taught when children are in the third grade in some schools.

Notes: 1) mandate 命令   2) convenient 方便的   3) expense 花費   4) transportation 交通 5) geography 地理

18 中國的中學教育情況如何？ What is the secondary education like in China?

Chinese secondary schools are called middle schools. They are divided into junior and senior levels. Both offer three-academic-year courses. Students begin their secondary education at the age of twelve, with most of them being non-board students.

Usually a regular middle school has two semesters, totalling nine months. Students study in school five days a week. Each day has seven classroom-teaching periods lasting 45 minutes. The academic curriculum consists of Chinese, mathematics, physics, chemistry, geology, foreign languages, history, geography, politics, physiology, music, fine arts, and physical education.Some middle schools also offer vocational subjects.

Since not all the students can be admitted into universities, the government attaches great importance to expanding vocational and technical schools to prepare students for jobs. The vocational education generally falls into three categories: junior secondary, senior secondary and tertiary education. Junior vocational education refers to the vocational and technical education after primary school education and is part of the Nine-Year Compulsory Education. The senior secondary category mainly refers to the vocational education at the level of senior high school education. Tertiary vocational education mainly enrolls graduates from regular high schools and secondary vocational schools. The schooling lasts two to three years and emphasizes vocational and technical training aimed at preparing students for work.

Notes: 1) academic 學術性的 2) non-board 非寄宿、走讀 3) semester 學期 4) physics 物理學 5) chemistry 化學 6) politics 政治 7) physiology 生理學 8) vocational 職業的 9) admit 接收 10) technical 技術的

19 中國的高等教育情況如何？ What is the higher education like in China?

Higher education at the undergraduate level includes two-year junior colleges and four-year colleges and universities. Many colleges and universities also offer graduate programs, leading to a Master's or PhD degree. To obtain a bachelor's degree, students are required to study four years; to obtain a master's degree, two or three years; and to obtain a PhD degree, three years.

Before 1989 all students who entered an institution of higher education were guaranteed employment upon graduation. Following 1989 students were no longer guaranteed employed. They instead needed to look for work and have their academic records scrutinized by prospective employers and then be interviewed by them. The practice of giving students some options in job-hunting is called "mutual selection" or "free marriage". In this case, graduating students as well as potential employers are now able to make their own choices. This helps ensure that both parties are satisfied.

Most Chinese universities and colleges are now engaged in international

academic exchanges in order to obtain a better understanding of higher education and scientific development abroad. At the same time, they are showing off China's achievements in these areas to the rest of the world.

Notes: 1) employment 就業 2) scrutinize 作詳細檢查 3) interview 面試 4) prospective 預期的；未來的 5) potential 潛在的

20 能談一談中國高考的情況嗎？ Can you say something about the college entrance examinations in China?

China's annual two-day college entrance examinations are held in June each year for enrollment in September. The enrollment of university students is based on moral, intellectual and physical qualities demonstrated by the national entrance examination results. In many schools students study from early morning to late at night, and classroom instruction is finished some six months prior to the college entrance examination in order to give their students time to prepare for the examination. The best first tier universities have first pick in recruiting students. Second and third tier universities recruit students afterwards.

Notes: 1) enrollment 入學 2) intellectual 智力的 3) tier 等級 4) recruit 徵募、吸收

21 你知道中國高校的學生宿舍情況嗎？ What are the dormitories like in Chinese universities and colleges?

Almost all dormitory buildings are located on university and college campuses. Campus dormitories are remarkably uniform in their outward appearance and furnishings, with communal shower rooms and laundry rooms.In many dormitories boiled water for drinking must be carried from a boiler room outside the dorm building.Although either four or eight students share a room in the dormitory, most students have found that with some imagination and effort, rooms can be decorated and arranged to suit individual tastes.

The dormitory community is cared by the shifu（師傅）, workers who clean the hallways and common rooms, distribute mail, and generally watch over dormitory residents and guests. Some of buildings have been built with better facilities, including private bathroom in each room.

Notes: 1) remarkably 引人注目地　2) uniform 統一的　3) outward 外面的　4) furnishing 設備　5) communal公用的　6) laundry 洗衣房　7) decorate 裝飾

22 中國大學生的社會關係的基本格局是怎樣的？
What is the basic pattern of social relationships among Chinese college students?

The pattern of social relationships among Chinese students tends to be tightly integrated into small groups. Most students in theses groups are both roommates and classmates. As classmates, the students go together as a group from class to class because their academic schedules are largely determined on a group basis. These class collectives are often stable over the three or four years. A Chinese student at a large university has little social contact with those who enter the institution simultaneously, even less with those who enter at other times. His or her social life is intensely focused on roommates and classmates doing the same coursework.

Notes: 1) integrate 結合　2) contact 接觸　3) simultaneously 同時地　4)intensely 極度地

23 學生為何又稱「桃李」？ Why are students also referred to as "peach and plum" in Chinese?

Taoli man tianxia（桃李滿天下）is a popular saying in China. It means "a teacher has students everywhere." Tao means "peach," and li "plum." Why do people use tao and li to imply "student"?

During the early Warring States Period there was a top-official at ministerial level under the State of Wei（魏國）whose name was Zizhi（子質）. During his official tenure, Zizhi used his superior position to give many people higher official positions and ranking.However, when he displeased the king and was removed from office, nobody came out and addressed the king as an advocate on behalf of Zizhi. Finally, Zizhi had to leave his country and went to the State of Zhao（趙國）.

One day Zizhi told the king of Zhao what happened to him in the State of Wei. He complained that those officials, who had been promoted as officials through his influence, had failed to plead on his behalf. Upon hearing of his story, the king began to console him with a following story.

He said, "If you grow peach and plum plants in spring, you will be able to sit under the shade of the plants for a rest in summer and pick up fruit from the trees in autumn. However, if you grow puncture vines in spring, you can't sit under the shade of the vines for a rest in summer and pick up fruits from them in autumn. Moreover, vines often prick with thorns."

On hearing the story from the king, Zizhi relaxed and relief grew on his face. Thus people later used peach and plum as a figure of speech for students.

Notes: 1) ministerial 部長的 2) tenure 占有期；任期 3) advocate 擁護 4) complain 抱怨 5) plead 懇求 6) console 安慰 7) puncture vine 蒺藜 8) prick 刺痛、刺傷 9) thorn 荊棘 10) a figure of speech 修辭、比喻

24 名落孫山是什麼意思？ What does mingluo Sun Shan mean?

Mingluo Sun Shan means "to fail in a competitive examination." Sun Shan（孫山）was a person in the Song Dynasty. One day when he was ready to depart for the provincial capital to take part in an imperial civil service exanimation, an old man in the same village visited him, inviting Sun Shan to go together with his son, who also was on the same mission. The old man expected Sun Shan to take care of his son during their stay in the capital. Sun Shan accepted the old man's invitation, and the two men left the village for their trip.

The two men arrived at the city and took the examination. Afterwards, they continued to stay in the capital, waiting for a written announcement stating which candidates had successfully passed the examination.

The day the examination results were announced, Sun Shan found his name on the list of those who passed, but he ranked last among these examinees. The man who came with him from the same village failed the examination. Being depressed, he continued to stay downtown for a few more days, while Sun Shan went back home alone.

After Sun Shan arrived at his village, he came across the old man who asked him if his son was on the list. Sun Shan responded with two poetic lines saying, "The last name on the list is Sun Shan, and your virtuous and able son stands even behind me（解名盡處是孫山，賢郎更在孫山外）."

Notes: 1) competitive 具有競爭性的　2) invitation 邀請　3) announcement 通告　4) examinee 應試者 5) depressed 沮喪的　6) respond 回答

飲食典故與趣談 Interesting Stories About Chinese Food

1 八寶豆腐 Eight Treasure Tofu

Originally, Eight Treasure Tofu was one of imperial dishes served during the reign of the Qing Dynasty Kangxi Emperor（清朝康熙年間）. Emperor Kangxi liked high quality dishes.Imperial cooks would satisfy Emperor Kangxi's taste with boneless chicken, duck, fish, and pork. Besides, the cooks also used soybeans to produce tender tofu, which was added into chicken soup with other minced ingredients until the soup became thick.The other ingredients included pork, chicken, shrimp, ham, dried mushrooms, melon seeds and pine nuts.

Emperor Kangxi ate the tofu soup. He was extremely satisfied with the food and noticed that the tofu soup both tasted really good and had nutritious ingredients that could prolong people's life. Emperor Kangxi therefore named the soup "Eight Treasure Tofu" because the soup contained eight nutritious ingredients. The emperor had an imperial scholar write down the imperial recipe and its cooking method.

Since the recipe was a valuable treasure, the emperor at times granted the recipe to his favourite officials. According to ancient documents, Emperor Kangxi arrived in Hangzhou during his inspection tour to South China. Governor Song Muzhong（宋牧仲）hosted Emperor Kangxi in Hangzhou. In return, the emperor kindly granted him the Eight Treasure Tofu recipe. Overwhelmed by the unexpected

favour, Song Muzhong kept it only to himself as his most valuable treasure.

Later, Emperor Kangxi passed the same invaluable recipe to another official named Xu Xueqian（徐學乾）. Finally Wang Mengting（王孟亭）received the recipe. Since he served as "taishou"（mayor，太守）, the tofu soup was also called "Wang Tai shou Eight Treasure Tofu"（王太守八寶豆腐）during the reign of the Qing Dynasty Qianlong Emperor（乾隆年間）.

One day, a famous gourmet cook whose name was Yuan Mei（袁枚）visited Mayor Wang at his home where he tasted the Eight Treasure Tofu. Afterwards he wrote down the recipe in his book called Menus of the Su Garden（《隨園食單》）. Since then, this recipe gradually spread among common people and thus became a well-known dish in Hangzhou.

Notes: 1) originally 起初　2) reign 在位期間　3) boneless 無骨的　4) mince 切碎　5) nutritious 有營養的　6) prolong 延長　7) recipe 食譜　8) invaluable 非常貴重的　9) gourmet 美食家

2 臭豆腐　Smelly Tofu

During the reign of the Qing Dynasty Kangxi Emperor there lived a scholar named Wang Zhihe（王致和）who was from Xianyuan County, Anhui Province. Wang once went to the capital city where he took part in the imperial exams. Afterwards Wang had to stay in Beijing and earned a living by making tofu. He learned this skill from his parents while he was growing up.

In the beginning of his tofu business Wang planned to make money to pay for his trip back to his hometown in Anhui.As days went by, Wang decided to continue his tofu business in Beijing. One summer he needed money for his son's marriage. His whole family planned to produce as much tofu as possible, hoping that their efforts would enable them to earn enough money for the coming marriage.

Unfortunately, very few shoppers went there for tofu. Wang worried that his tofu might go bad as the temperature is high in summer.

After thinking long and hard, suddenly an idea came to Wang's mind. To reduce the possibility that the tofu would go bad, he decided to do the following: cut the tofu into small cubes, then sprinkle some salt and Chinese prickly ash powder on the tofu's surface and finally store all of it in a small inner hall.

A few days later, Wang's family smelt something unusual coming from the hall. Wang went there, and to his surprise, his white-colored tofu had all turned into another kind of tofu. Each piece remained in the same shape, but its color appeared qing（青）, a bluish-greenish hue. He picked up one piece and tasted it. "Well," he said, "I have made tofu all my life, but I have never tasted anything like this before." Overjoyed, Wang moved all the qing-colored tofu out of the hall and displayed them outside his shop for sale. At the same time, he hung up a signboard, which said, "Qing-colored tofu has a unique flavor and a strong smell（臭中有奇香的青方）."

People passing by saw this new kind of tofu on sale. Out of curiosity, some people bought pieces to have a try. News about the qing-colored tofu spread far and wide. As a result, Wang sold out all his preserved tofu in less than half a day.

One midnight, when Empress Dowager Cixi（慈禧太后）began eating a meal, she suddenly wanted to eat steamed corn bread with preserved tofu on it. So her servant went to Wang's shop to purchase the qing-colored tofu for Dowager Cixi. Because Dowager Cixi liked the preserved tofu from Wang's shop, the reputation of Wang styled qing-colored tofu spread rapidly. Towards the end of the Qing Dynasty, lots of his smelly tofu was being sold throughout Beijing.

Notes: 1) temperature 溫度　2) prickly ash 花椒　3) signboard 招牌 4)preserved 醃製的

3 麻婆豆腐 Braised Mapo Tofu

Mapo Tofu（stewed bean curd with minced beef or pork，麻婆豆腐）is a common Sichuan dish.

Legend has it that toward the end of the Xianfeng reign of the Qing Dynasty（清代咸豐末年）, there was a market named Wanfu Bridge（萬福橋）in the suburbs outside Chengdu's North Gate. Every morning, many businessmen and shoppers went there to buy things. Near the market lived a couple who owned an inn, selling simple meals and tea.The husband's family name was Chen（陳）, and his wife was called Chen Mapo（陳麻婆）. Mapo usually refers to a lady with the pockmarked face. The lady was skilled in cooking tasty dishes, and her tofu dish was especially well known.

Chen Mapo and her husband carefully selected soybeans, and she never used stale beans for tofu. The water they used to soak beans was from a well near the river, which had a natural sand filter that guaranteed high quality water. When coagulating bean paste into solid tofu, they used the coagulant from the northern area between Shanxi（陝西）and Gansu（甘肅）. When cooking, she used the bean paste sauce produced in Pixian County, Sichuan Province（郫縣豆瓣）.

At that time oil peddlers usually carried poles on their shoulders as they walked towards Chengdu City. On either side of each pole was a basket that contained oil. When the peddlers passed by the small inn owned by the couple, they would stop to eat their meal there. Sometimes the peddlers ladled out a few spoonfuls of oil out of their oil baskets to offer to the couple.

After selling their oil in the city, they returned home with a little leftover oil in their empty baskets. On the way, the peddlers would purchase some beef and stop at the inn again. They gave beef and the leftover oil to Mapo who then braised tofu with these items. The other ingredients she added included fermented soybeans, bean paste sauce, and dry hot pepper. When the bean curd was well done, Mapo sprinkled some numb pepper powder on the top of the food, which smelled fragrant and tasted numb and spicy.

Gradually the inn's business flourished because of the reputation of Mapo's tofu. Many other customers followed suit by taking edible oil and beef to the inn, hoping that Mapo might cook the similar tofu dish with the same ingredients.

Later, her customers named her cooked tofu as "Mapo Tofu" after her pockmarked face. A book called The Overall View of Chengdu (《成都通覽》) was published during the reign of the Qing Dynasty Guangxu Emperor (清光緒年間). The book states that the Mapo's inn as well as her tofu dish had become famous.

Up to the 1920's the inn continued to stick to its traditional method of cooking Mapo Tofu, and still remained unadorned as it was before, with old-fashioned square tables and high-legged stools. As usual, when customers entered the inn, they would borrow a rice bowl from the inn and go to stores nearby to purchase rapeseed oil and beef. Then they would return to the inn and sit at a table to wait patiently for their Mapo Tofu dishes to be ready.Some customers might order from other stores nearby a cup of wine and some other extra dishes to go with Mapo Tofu like fried peanuts, beans, and salted or stewed pork in soy sauce.

During the War of Resistance Against Japan, many people immigrated to Chengdu. With the growing population, various northern and southern styled restaurants emerged in Chengdu. From 1935, the inn began to offer a larger variety of dishes to attract more customers. Despite of the change, the inn's main dish remained Mapo Tofu.

In the early 1940s, the old inn displayed a new signboard "Chen Styled Mapo Tofu (陳麻婆豆腐)." Meanwhile, the inn owner modernized the inn's facilities in order to provide full course meals. After 1949 the Chen Styled Mapo Tofu

Restaurant moved to downtown Chengdu where it remains today.

After the War of Resistance Against Japan, the immigrants who had fled to Chengdu returned to where they came from and took Chen Styled Mapo Tofu recipe with them. These people gradually spread Mapo Tofu throughout the country.

In 1982 chefs from Chen Styled Mapo Tofu Restaurant were invited to lecture on Sichuanese cuisine in Japan. Japanese gourmets gathered to view how Mapo Tofu was cooked in a traditional Chinese way.

Chen Styled Mapo Tofu has won a several honours for its taste. In 1990 the Chen Styled Mapo Tofu Sichuan Food Restaurant（陳麻婆川菜館）won the Golden Cooking Vessel Prize（《金鼎獎》）at the national level, and in 1992 the restaurant awarded the title of "The Famous Brand（著名商標）" by the Sichuan Provincial Industrial and Commercial Bureau. In 1993 the title "China's Time-Honoured Brand（中華老字號）" was granted to the restaurant by China's Ministry of Trade and in 2002 Chen Styled Mapo Tofu was honored as a Chinese Famous Dish（中國名菜）.

The Chen Styled Mapo Tofu Sichuan Food Restaurant has now produced a kind of Mapo sauce paste that is packaged into small bags and sold on markets to meet increasing demand from customers. Currently there is a chain of Chen Styled Mapo Tofu Restaurants in Chengdu, Beijing, and Tokyo, and their unique paste attracts customers in and outside of China.

Notes: 1) legend 傳奇 2) suburb 市郊 3) pockmarked 有麻子的 4) filter 過濾器 5) guarantee 保證 6) coagulant 凝結劑 7) peddler 小販 8) ladle 長勺；用長勺舀 9) spoonful 一匙的量 10) flourish 興旺 11) unadorned 未經裝飾的 12) old-fashioned 老式的 13) rapeseed 油菜子 14) immigrate 移居 15) vessel 容器、器皿 16) time-honoured 歷史悠久的

4 魚香肉絲 Fish-Flavored Shredded Pork

Yuxiang wei（魚香味）literally means "fish-flavored sauce." The sauce is a mixture of seasonings that usually consists of red chilli pepper, spring onions, ginger, garlic, sugar, salt, soy sauce, among other ingredients. The sauce tends to be salty, sweet, sour, and fragrant. On restaurant menus this sauce is often translated as "hot garlic sauce." As we can see that the dish contains no fish ingredients. The reason why it is called "fish-flavoured" is because the sauce was usually used to cook fish. The following legend tells us how it began to be used to cook pork.

A long time ago, there was a business family in Sichuan. The whole family enjoyed eating fish. When cooking fish, they would add some spring onions, ginger, garlic, wine, vinegar, and soy sauce to remove the unpleasant fish smell.

One evening, when the family hostess was stir frying shredded pork, she added all the leftover seasonings from her fish cooking. She had thought that this dish might not taste good because the seasonings might not suit pork.

A moment later, her husband returned home from his business. He went directly to the food table where he picked up chopsticks, grasped the food from that dish and tasted it. Having found the food surprisingly tasty, the husband cheerfully asked his wife how this dish was cooked. The wife then told him that she used the leftover seasonings for the fish to cook pork. Afterwards the family named the sauce as "Fish-flavoured Sauce".

In 1909 a book called The Overall View of Chengdu（《成都通覽》）was published. The book had of 1, 328 Sichuan cooking recipes, but did not include any fish-flavored dishes. The absence of such recipes shows that fish-flavored dishes appeared only after 1909. Sichuan-style menus currently contain a list of fish-flavored dishes, including the Fish-flavored Eggplant（魚香茄子）, Fish-flavored Pork Liver（魚香豬肝）, Fish-flavored Pork Kidney（魚香腰子）, and Fish-flavored Shredded Pork（魚香肉絲）.

Notes: 1) shred 切碎 2) chilli pepper 辣椒 3) spring onion 蔥 4) ginger 姜

5) garlic 蒜　6) seasoning 作料　7) leftover 剩餘的　8) cheerfully 愉快地　9) recipe菜譜　10) eggplant 茄子　11) liver 肝

5 泡菜魚火鍋　Fish Hotpot with Pickled Vegetables

Paocai（泡菜）means "pickled vegetables" and paocai yu huoguo（泡菜魚火鍋）means "fish hotpot with pickled vegetable."

Sichuan local pickles are basic ingredients of hotpot. Traditionally every local family in Sichuan enjoys keeping a large earthen jar or container at home to make family-style pickled vegetables. To produce pickles, place peppercorn and salt in a clean container with boiling water. Add wine, ginger, and hot pepper (cut into small pieces) into the container after the water is cool. Cut turnips, carrots, and cucumbers into small pieces approximately the size of a small finger, and place them in salt water. Some more vegetables and chicken claws may be added. Then cover the container with a tight fitting lid and let the vegetables soak for about two or three days. Pickles are not only a daily dish, but are also presented even at formal banquets.

Hotpot originated in Chongqing and it is known for its peppery and spicy taste. Numerous sidewalk hotpot stalls and exquisite hotpot restaurants have been set up to meet the increasing customer demand. Restaurants offer various kinds of hotpot to suit customers' tastes.

The "Fish Hotpot with Pickled Vegetable" can be traced back to the invention of a kind of hot pot known as Chuanjiang Haozi Fish Hotpot（川江號子魚火鍋）.

A long time ago riverboats had no mechanical gear to navigate along Yangtze River. When a boat went up stream through the narrow stretches of the gorges, trackers sometimes had to wade through rapids or along the shore of the river, pulling the boat with a rope, while boatmen wielded bamboo iron-hooked poles.

One day a boat named "Chuanjiang Hao（川江號）" travelled up stream along Yangtze River. When the boat reached the stretches of the gorges, the boatmen and trackers could not go further due to fatigue and hunger. They instead all laid down on the ground to rest.

The boat captain had a boatman anchor the boat and ordered the cook to prepare meat dishes for the fatigued men. Unfortunately, the cook had nothing to cook on board, so the captain picked up his fishing net and spread it into the river. A moment later, he caught enough fish to fill up several barrels.

The cook cleaned the fish and boiled soup in a wok that contained several seasonings like spicebush oil（山胡椒油）, spices, and pickled ginger and peppers. Then he added the fish and re-boiled the fish soup until it was well cooked. The tired men gathered together, eating the fish and soup from the wok. Meanwhile some other boats passed by, and their passengers and boatmen were also invited to come on board and taste this food. This fish soup was later named Chuanjiang Hao Fish Hotpot after the boat's name.

Fish hotpot with pickled vegetables still remains one of the most popular hotpots, and traditional restaurants are usually full of customers every day wanting to try it. Especially on weekends, customers may have to wait in line outside restaurants before having hotpot. While waiting, customers eat watermelon seeds and drink tea.

Notes: 1) hotpot 火鍋 2) peppercorn 乾胡椒 3) turnip 蘿蔔 4) carrot 胡蘿蔔 5) cucumber 黃瓜 6) approximately 大約 7) banquet 宴會 8) gear 傳動裝置 9) navigate 航行 10) tracker 縴夫 11) wade 蹚 12) rapids 急流 13) wield 揮舞 14) fatigue 疲勞 15) barrel 桶 16) wok 鐵鍋

6 東坡肉　Dongpo Meat

When Su Dongpo served as the prefecture governor of Hangzhou, he had a dam built across West Lake. The project sought to dredge the lake so that farmers could better use it to irrigate their fields.

One day during the Spring Festival many local people visited Su Dongpo at his home, and wished him Happy New Year. They took pork and wine to show their thanks for his lake construction efforts. Su accepted the gifts and had someone cut the pork into small cube-shaped pieces and braised in soy sauce. When the red braised pork was ready, he sent it out to the families of the labourers who had worked on the West Lake construction project.

At that time there was a large local restaurant near where the owner saw everybody praise the cube-shaped pork braised by Su Dongpo. He had his cooks cut and braise pork in the same way in order to sell it in his restaurant as "Dongpo Meat." Soon after the creation of this new dish, the restaurant's business grew dramatically. Later other restaurants followed suit, thus spreading this dish far and wide.

Today this dish is still popular in Sichuan restaurants across the country.

Notes: 1) prefecture 府、專區 2) dredge 疏濬（河道） 3) cube 立方形 4) dramatically 戲劇性地；顯著地

7 東坡肘子 Dongpo Stewed Pork Shoulder

The Dongpo Zhouzi Dish refers to the Dongpo-Style Stewed Pork Shoulder, the upper part of a pork leg, in Sichuan Cuisine. This heavy dish has lots of fat but is easy to digest and very tasty.Many people who visit Sichuan or eat in a Sichuan restaurant prefer ordering order this dish. Why is the dish named after Su Dongpo, the great Song Dynasty writer?

Su Dongpo (also known as Su Shi，蘇東坡）was a remarkably accomplished ancient Chinese writer. Apart from Su's literary achievements, he also created several dishes throughout his life. He even made wine, cooked snacks, and revised the folk menu. Based on his experience, he wrote some culinary essays, including Ode to Vegetables and Roots（《菜根賦》）, Song of Pork（《豬肉頌》）, and Song of Dongpo Soup（《東坡羹頌》）. Among these dishes, the Dongpo-style Stewed Pork Shoulder is well known across China.

After Su Dongpo passed the Jinshi examination（metropolitan exams, administered in the capital every three years, 進士科考）in 1061, he was appointed notary in Fengxiang（鳳翔府）, but his official career was marked by a series of political setbacks. In his forty-year career as a government official, Su Dongpo was exiled politically on three occasions. In 1079 Su Dongpo was imprisoned for two years after being accused of slandering the imperial court with his poems. After being pardoned, he went to Huangzhou（黃州）, Hubei Province, where he continued to work for the local government.But because Su's new position was in name only and carried very little responsibility, his salary was greatly reduced.

Because his income was so low, Su had difficulties supporting his family, so at the beginning of each month he would divide his salary into 30 portions and hang them up on a house beam. Each day he would take down one portion from the beam to be used for his family's daily necessities.

By the end of each day Su Dongpo would store any surplus in a thick bamboo stick, and would usually use such savings to buy wine for hosting guests. During his stay in Huangzhou, Su Dongpo found that local people disliked eating pork and that local pork was generally very cheap, so he often purchased pork to cook at home according to the method from Meishan County in Sichuan Province（四川眉山）where he was born.

He wrote in his Song of Pork（《豬肉頌》）:

In Huangzhou good pork is produced,

And it is as cheap as the earth.

The local rich families dislike eating pork,

And the poor know little about the pork cooking.

As you prepare a pork food,

Control the fire at a low temperature,

Add small amounts of water,

It will be very delicious when it's brewed long enough.

Every day when I get up, I fill two bowls

With the cooked pork to satisfy my family,

And other people don't necessarily care about it.

（黃州好豬肉，價賤如泥土。富者不肯吃，貧者不解煮。慢著火，少著水，火候足時它自美。每日起來打兩碗，飽得自家君莫管。）

In this poem Su Dongpo shows how to prepare the pork shoulder emphasizing the fire temperature and cooking method. With his help, many people in Huangzhou started learning how to cook this dish, enabling it to spread far and wide.

The following are two more stories about the origin of this dish.

According to the first story, once Su Dongpo visited Yongxiu area in Jiangxi Province（江西永修）where he cured a local farmer's ill child. The child's father prepared a meal to express his appreciation for his son's medical treatment. Su Dongpo accepted the offer.

While waiting for the meal, Su looked around the rural scenery. He couldn't help reciting, "Rice straw with sparkling dew smell fragrant to my heart's content（禾草珍珠透心香）." The farmer who was cooking the pork in the kitchen misheard it as "It smells fragrant to my heart's content if you boil the pork with rice straw（和草整煮透心香）." "He is teaching me how to cook this dish," he thought. Then the farmer boiled the big piece of pork as a whole with the rice straw that was used to tie the meat.Unexpectedly the cooked pork brought out a pleasant flavor.

Chinese characters are neither alphabetical nor phonetic. The same sound may represent different characters of totally different meanings. Consider, for example, these characters. "禾" and "和" have the same sound. However, "禾" refers to "rice" and "和" means "together with" "珍珠" and "整煮" have similar sounds, but the first two characters as a phrase means "pearls" and the latter "boil together with something whole." So it is no surprise that the farmer misunderstood what Su Dongpo said when heard him chanting poetry.

According to the second story, the Stewed Pork Shoulder dish was actually created by Su Dongpo's wife rather than Su Dongpo himself. One day his wife stewed a pork shoulder. To her surprise, the stewed pork skin turned brown and clung to the pot because she had forgotten to add more water to the pot. She had no choice but to add various seasonings to re-stew the pork shoulder, wishing that her second cooking would drive away the burnt smell. Unexpectedly the lightly brown pork was very tasty when Su Dongpo ate it.Afterwards he continued to improve the dish before he recommended this dish to his friends and neighbors.

Notes: 1) stew 炖 2) shoulder 帶肩肉的前腿肉 3) remarkably 明顯地 4) accomplished 熟練 5) achievement 成就 6) notary 公證人、判官 7) slander 誹謗 8) responsibility 責任 9) portion 一份 10) necessity 必要性 11) emphasize 強調 12) cling to 依附

8 宮保雞丁 Chicken Stir-Fried with Nuts and Chilli Pep-pers

Stir-fried Chicken with Peanuts is also known Gongbao Chicken. The main ingredients for this dish are chicken breast and peanuts. Most people believe that this dish falls under the category of Sichuanese cooking. Legend has it that Ding Baozhen（丁寶楨）invented this dish while serving as governor of Sichuan Province during the Qing Dynasty.

However, local people in Shandong Province disagree, saying that Ding Baozhen invented this dish while serving as governor of Shandong. For this reason, Gongbao Chicken is also considered a Shandong recipe.

People from Beijing have another opinion. Gongbao Chicken was allegedly on the list of imperial banquet courses during the Qing Dynasty, and this tradition may lead us to believe that this dish originated as an imperial style cuisine.

Lastly, local people in Guizhou Province take issue with all the above accounts. There is a story that says that Guizhou was Ding Baozhen's home province. Once he returned to Guizhou for a short visit to his parents. When he arrived home, his relatives and friends entertained him with dinner. Among the dinner courses was a fried cubed chicken with green pepper, which overwhelmed Ding Baozhen. He immediately asked for the name of this dish. Someone attempted to please him by saying, "This dish is specially cooked for Your Excellence, and its name is 'Gongbao Chicken.'" "Gongbao" was Ding's emeritus official title.According to this story, local people in Guizhou believe that Gongbao Chicken is one of their home province's local dishes.

Well, according to the history book, Ding Baozhen's hometown was Pingyuan（平遠）, Guizhou. In 1853 he passed the highest imperial examinations, and in 1867 Ding was appointed governor of Shandong Province. During his tenure in office he had few social contacts and didn't care what his residence looked like. However, he loved good food. When Ding was not carrying out his official responsibilities, he would take off his official dress, put on common clothes and go out on a tour in search of great food. These outings surely gave him the chance to taste Stewed Prawns with Brown Sauce（紅燒大蝦）, Stir-fried Pig Tripe and Kidney（油爆雙脆）, Spicy Braised Pig Intestines（九轉大腸）, and other tasty local dishes.

One day Ding put on his usual common clothes and left his government office with his servant. They toured the Daming Lake（大明湖）. The two enjoyed the gentle breeze and green willow trees around the lake. It was mid-noon when Ding walked into a peasant's courtyard where there was an elderly lady feeding chickens.

The people of Jinan（濟南）were traditionally known for their hospitality, so the woman ushered them in a living room where she offered them cups of tea. At the same time, she had someone get her son back from a restaurant where he worked as a cook.The son could judge from Ding's imposing appearance and his different accent that he was an important guest.

Ding chatted with the woman while his son cooked for them in the kitchen. Ding was hungry, but he had to wait because the meal was very carefully prepared. He had been afraid that the meal prepared by the farmer's son might not be tasty. A moment later, a delicious smell wafted into the living room from the kitchen. The woman's son came in carrying a tray that contained a few dishes.

The son laid the table and stood aside. The woman smiled, inviting Ding to eat with her together. One of the dishes caught his attention.Ding quickly used his chopsticks to grasp a cubed thing from that dish and then put it into his mouth. His tongue immediately felt a little bit numb. As he chewed the food, the food was crisply tender and tasty. The food pleased Ding so well that it was beyond his powers of description.

"What is the name of the dish?" Ding asked the man.

"Fried Cubed Chicken." said the son with a smile.

"Why does it taste so tender?" Ding asked with curiosity.

"The meat was taken from the chicken breast. I diced the meat into cubes, coated them in starch paste. Then I quickly fried the coated meat in heated cooking oil at medium temperature. Afterward I added peanuts and numb pepper, and stir-fried them with the meat at a high temperature for a second."

Ding nodded. He took a peanut out from the plate with his chopsticks, put it into his mouth, and chewed it in appreciation. After the meal, Ding returned to his office. He soon employed the man to cook for his family because this meal impressed him so much. Afterwards, whenever Ding held a banquet to entertain his guests, he would arrange his cook to make the fried chicken to please them.

Ding later was transferred to work in Sichuan where he also brought his cook. During his stay there, the cook continued preparing the fried chicken dish. Later, his descendants made Sichuan-style fried chicken with hot instead of numb peppers.Sichuan people treasure hot pepper taste. Sichuan has a humid climate that encourages people to eat very spicy food, and the red pepper may help them feel less damp inside.

After Ding passed away, a local Sichuan official presented to the emperor the recipe of Fried Chicken with Peanuts known as Gongbao Chicken. This recipe was later placed on the list of famous imperial dishes. Gradually it spread far and wide to other parts of China.

Notes: 1) breast 胸部　2) category 種類　3) take issue with 提出異議　4) emeritus 退休後保留頭銜的　5) residence 住宅　6) outing 郊遊　7) prawn 對蝦　8) tripe（牛等的）肚（供食用）9) kidney 腎　10) intestine 腸　11) hospitality 殷勤款待　12) crisply 酥脆地　13) starch 澱粉　14) stir-fry 炒　15) transfer 調任　16) descendant 後裔

9 乾菜鴨子　Braised Duck with Dried Vegetables

Braised Duck with Dried Vegetables is a traditional dish in Jiande（建德）, Zhejiang Province. Its origin relates to Emperor Qianlong's inspection tour of South China（乾隆南巡）in the Qing Dynasty.

While passing through the regions along the lower reaches of Yangtze River, the emperor noticed that there were many ducks swimming in rivers and lakes.

Near lunchtime, the emperor unexpectedly asked his cook to single out a duck to prepare the meal. The cook quickly slaughtered a duck but did not have enough time to take out some feathery skin.

At his wits' end, the cook braised the duck together with many dried vegetables. These vegetables were black in color, wrapping up the duck skin so that the emperor could not see the feathers.

Finally the cook presented this dish to the emperor who highly praised it. The Braised Duck with Dried Vegetables dish arose out of this incident.

Notes: 1) inspection tour 考察旅行 2) single out 挑選 3) feathery 長著羽毛的

10 爆鱔卷 Stir-Fry Yellow Eel at High Temperature

Stir-fried Yellow Eel is a flavored dish, which has the yellow eel as its main ingredient. The eel appears curved through the stir-frying process at high temperature and tastes tender and fresh. Behind the dish is a folk story explaining why people eat the eel.

A long time ago, according to legend, there was a yellow snake in Yunmeng Large Pool（雲夢大澤）, who could speed across the sky and had magical powers. The snake developed his power in the hope that, at some future date, he could attain the dao（道）and be transformed into a splendid dragon palace for eternity.

Once the snake went to an assembly attended by thousand celestial beings for the pilgrimage to Guanyin（the Goddess of Mercy，觀音）. He expected Guanyin to allow him to obtain the dao at an early stage.

Guanyin saw through his purpose when he had an audience with her. However, in line with her perfect compassion and kindness, Guanyin required the snake to do good things and accumulate as many charitable and pious deeds as possible within three years to be able to ascend into the circle where the celestial beings resided.Guanyin also offered the snake dan（丹）, a magic cinnabar pill, allowing the snake to turn into a human being to carry out the assignment.

The yellow snake swallowed the bill and soon turned into a rich man. He called himself Lord Huang. In the beginning, he abided by law and behaved well. However, as days went by, he abandoned Guanyin's advice, gradually revealing his sly nature by joining forces with evil local gentry and ruffians to bully poor people. In order to cover up his misdeeds, his accomplices hanged up a golden inscribed board that said "Obtain great happiness in doing charitable deeds（為善最樂）."

There was an honest scholar who couldn't tolerate Lord Huang' bad deeds. He secretly said to others, "The board's inscription will reveal reality if 人, a Chinese character radical is added to the left side of 為."

Chinese characters is usually composed of two parts, a left part and a right part, or a top part and a bottom part. When the radical（人）is added to the component（為）, it becomes another character（偽）, which means "false." Wei（偽）and Shan（善）form a phrase, which means "hypocritical." The new inscription reads "Obtain great happiness in being hypocritical（偽善最樂）."

Upon hearing of what the scholar said, Lord Huang immediately arrested the scholar's whole family and tortured them. Lord Huang even attempted to rape the scholar's daughter.

At this very moment, Guanyin arrived at the spot and said, "To be a dragon or a celestial being is for you wishful thinking. From now on, any human being can slaughter you for a dish（成龍登仙你妄想，任人宰殺當菜吃）."

Notes: 1) eel 鱔魚 2) magical 魔法的 3) eternity 永恆 4) have an audience with 觀見 5) compassion 同情 6) accumulate 積累 7) charitable 慈善的 8) pious 虔誠的 9) ascend 上升 10) celestial beings 神仙 11) cinnabar 硃砂 12) assignment 任務 13) sly 狡詐的 14) gentry 紳士 15) ruffian 惡棍 16) misdeed 罪行 17) hypocritical 偽善的 18) torture 施以酷刑；折磨

11 佛跳牆 Buddha Jumps over the Wall

Fo Tiao Qian（佛跳牆，Buddha jumps over the wall）is an unusual name of a complex Fuzhou stockpot（福州）that has as many as 30 ingredients, including chicken, ham, pork, shark's fin, scallops, abalone, vegetables, and seasonings.The stockpot appeared in the late Qing Dynasty and was named "Braised Eight Delicacies in the Jar（壇燒八寶）" and was later renamed "Full Happiness and Longevity（福壽全）", but finally was called "Fo Tiao Qian." One thing deserves to be mentioned: Fo Tiao Qian and Fu Shou Quan sound extremely close in Mandarin influenced by Fuzhou dialect.

There are several stories concerning the origins of Fo Tiao Qian.

According to the first story, a little monk lived in a Buddhist monastery a long time ago. One day a senior monk found him eating meat behind other monks. The little monk immediately ran away and jumped over the monastery's wall with his meat jar.

According to the second story, once a beggar carried a broken earthen jar, begging for food on the street. After he received some leftover food and wine from a restaurant, he put everything into his jar and re-cooked it on the street.An unusual aroma drifted from his cooking jar, and passers-by named it "the Stewed Assorted

Food." A restaurant boss had his cooks produce the food just as the beggar had done. These cooks added to the jar some other ingredients and cooking wine to enrich the flavor of the dish.

According to the third version, this food was created by the wife whose husband worked in the local financial office in Fuzhou during the Qing Dynasty. Once she prepared a home-dinner to host a high-ranking official invited by her husband. She put chicken, duck, pork, and cooking wine into a jar and stewed it at a low temperature. Her homemade food overwhelmed the distinguished guest who returned home and required his cook, Zheng Chunfa（鄭春發）, to learn how to cook this dish. Zheng further improved on it by adding more varied seafood, which he called "Braised Eight Delicacies in a Jar（壇燒八寶）."

Zheng later opened up his own restaurant and renamed this braised food "Full Happiness and Longevity." He even listed it as the number one dish of his restaurant. One scholar who ate in the restaurant couldn't help but compose an ode, which says, "壇啟葷香飄四鄰，佛聞棄禪跳牆來", literally meaning "When I opened the jar, the meat aroma reached everyone in the neighborhood.It smelled so good that a Buddhist monk ceased his meditation and jumped over the wall for the dish."

Notes: 1) complex 複合物　2) stockpot 湯罐　3) fin 鰭　4) scallop 扇貝　5) longevity 長壽　6) earthen 土製的　7) passer-by 過路人　8) high-ranking 高級的　9) delicacy 精美　10) meditation 冥想

12 涮羊肉　Instant-Boiled Mutton

Instant-Boiled Mutton is well known in Beijing. There are different stories regarding its origin.

According to the first story, Wang Shichong（王世充）of the Sui Dynasty proclaimed himself King of the State of Zheng（稱帝即位，國號鄭）and fought a hard battle in the Luoyang（洛陽）area against the army led by Li Shimin（李世民）for supremacy over the country. Li concentrated almost all of his soldiers and generals around Luoyang, and only ten men stayed with him on snow-covered Mt.Beimang（北邙山）. To his great surprise, Li soon found himself encircled by Wang's army. Even worse, he had no way at all to send an urgent message to his main force for help.

Although Wang's soldiers encircled Li and his small group, they were afraid to move forward to capture him. These soldiers thought that crafty Li might have laid a trap for them to fall in. Wang Shichong sent Shan Xiongxin（單雄信）to go up to meet Li to arrange a cease-fire.

Li received Shan, but he refused to promise the cease-fire.However, Li said, "General, if you sincerely want a cease-fire, could you let me think it through? I will reply to you tomorrow morning." Li continued, "General, I'd like to borrow your fur overcoat for our stay overnight on the hill; otherwise we will all freeze to death here."

Shan accepted Li's proposals.At night, a wild goat passed by the camp where Li and his soldiers stayed. The soldiers caught the goat for food. Li thought that bulky pieces of mutton would not be well cooked within a short time. So he had his soldiers chip mutton into thin slices, pierce through each slice with sticks and dip it into boiling water until it was well done. The soldiers followed Li's advice and ate well-boiled sliced mutton. Afterwards Li and his soldiers put on the fur overcoats and pretended to be a patrol team under Wang's army. They walked down the hill and through snowfields and successfully escaped from the Wang's surrounding encampment. Li later called the mutton they ate Instant Boiled Mutton.

According to the second story, Kublai Khan（忽必烈）once went with his main army forces on a southern expedition. One day the entire force was exhausted

after a long journey, so Kublai Khan ordered his soldiers to stop for a rest and prepare a meal. He also asked his cook to stew mutton for him.

His cook slaughtered a few sheep, and when he was cutting mutton, a scout arrived and reported to Kublai Khan, "The enemy troops are approaching."

Kublai Khan immediately ordered his force to move forward to the battlefield while shouting to his cook, "Mutton! Mutton!"

His cook quickly cut mutton into thin slices, put them in boiling water, and stirred them a little bit. He then dragged them out into a bowl, sprinkling some salt on the boiled mutton before he presented it to Kublai Khan.

Kublai Khan ate the mutton and then jumped onto his horse, rushing to the battlefield.After he won the battle, he held a feast to celebrate the victory and ordered the same sliced mutton food.

This time his cook chipped tender mutton into thin slices, adding other ingredients to improve its flavor. The cook said to Kublai Khan, "This dish has no name yet. Please bestow a name on this dish."

Kublai Khan replied with a smile, "Let's call it Instant-Boiled Mutton."

Notes: 1) instant 即刻的 2) proclaim 宣布 3) supremacy 最高權力 4) crafty 狡猾的 5) overcoat 大衣 6) proposal 提議 7) bulky 體積大的 8) encampment 紮營地 9) slaughter 屠殺

13 閉門羹 Bimen Thick Soup

Bimen means "to lock or close a door." When a guest visits someone else's home and finds the entrance door locked out, he or she is said be bimen geng, which means "denied entry."

Geng（羹）originally referred to a thick meat soup simmered at a low temperature, but later referred to a kind of meatless thick soup, including White Fungus Soup（銀耳羹）, Eatable Bird-Nest Soup（燕窩羹）and others. What is the relationship between bimen thick soup and being "denied entry?"

According to a story from the Tang Dynasty, there was a lady named Shi Feng（史鳳）. She was a well-known prostitute for her beautiful appearance and artistic pursuits, such as the lute, chess, calligraphy, and painting.

However, Shi Feng cared too much about social position and wealth and therefore despised people of lower social position. While hosting men, she usually divided visitors into upper, middle, and lower classes. An upper class visitor would stay in a perfumed room with lotus-patterned lights and pillows stitched with beautiful birds. A middle class visitor was offered a red-coloured quilt and a fragrant pillow. As for lower class visitors, Shi Feng herself never went out to meet them. Instead she had someone provide the visitor with a bowl of thick soup to suggest the visitor should leave.

At that time Shi Feng's courteous way to refuse visitors became one of the most popular topics among common people. The rumor gradually spread far and wide and thus the word "bimen thick soup" became synonymous with being "denied entry."

Notes: 1) fungus 菌類植物 2) prostitute 妓女 3) pursuit 事務 4) lotus 蓮（花） 5) courteous 有禮貌的；謙恭的 6) synonymous 同義的

14 臘八粥 Laba Rice Congee

The twelfth lunar month, or the last month in Chinese Lunar Calender, is called the month of la and ba means eight or the eighth. So Laba refers to the the eighth day of the month of la.

The Laba Festival is a Buddhist holiday. In ancient times in places where the

Han people lived, it was believed to be the day Sakyamuni attained immortality. So on that day, scriptures were chanted at monasteries and festive rice congee was prepared as offerings to Buddha.

There is an interesting story about Laba Rice Congee. Before Sakyamuni became the Buddha, he visited many mountains and rivers in India, meeting abbots and men of unusual calibre in quest of the true meaning of life. On the eighth day of the last lunar month, he came near a river in the state of Magadha（now Bihar State，今比哈爾邦）in North India, he collapsed on the ground in a deserted place, since he was exhausted and hungry. And then a shepherdess came who fed him with her own lunch and water that she had drawn up from a fountain. The lunch was actually a mixture of leftovers in her family kitchen for the last few days. It mainly consisted of various cereals, glutinous rice, dates, wild chestnuts, and fruits that she had collected on the mountain slope. The meal tasted better than anything to Sakyamuni, who had not had eaten for many days. After the meal, he had a bath in the river and sat under a bo tree to meditate. Here he became Buddha.

Since then, every year on that day, monks assemble to chant scriptures and give lectures on Buddhism. They also mark the occasion by eating sticky rice congee.

Monks in China have been eating Laba Rice Congee for more than a thousand years. Eating Laba Rice Congee became a widespread custom by the time of the Qing Dynasty. The royal family would bestow congee on ministers, officers, attendants, and palace maids. Today people still eat Laba Rice Congee on this holy day, but do so mainly because it's a seasonal specialty.

Notes: 1) festival 節日 2) immortality 不朽 3) congee粥 4) abbot 大寺院住持 5) calibre 品質 6) shepherdess 牧羊女 7) mixture 混合物 8) glutinous 黏稠的 9) chestnut 栗子 10) bo tree菩提樹 11) assemble 集合 12) scripture 經典；經文 13) specialty 特產

15 玉米粥進宮 How was Corn Porridge Introduced to the Imperial Palace?

According to folklore, the Qing Dynasty Kangxi Emperor（康熙皇帝）and his bodyguards once spent a whole day hunting on a mountain. When the sun was about to set, and the emperor was about to leave for home, a spotted deer passed by, and the emperor immediately spurred his horse to chase it. He quickly shot an arrow in an attempt to stop the running animal.

The emperor left his bodyguards far behind and was soon out of sight. He became lost as darkness fell. He continued to ride his horse, trying to join his bodyguards.

Soon afterwards the emperor saw a light far ahead. As he approached, the light turned out to be from a farmhouse. He got off the horse and walked into the house where a grey-haired old man and his sons were about to have dinner. On the dining table were pieces of steamed corn bread, a large bowl of corn porridge, and a dish of braised hare with mushroom.

The emperor felt hungry at the sight of the food on the table. He said, "I am a traveler, passing the mountain today. Could you offer me something to eat? I will pay you with silver."

Local mountain people there were known for being hospitable and thus invited him to sit at the table to eat.

After the dinner, the emperor said, "The dinner was delicious. Who made it?"

"I have three sons." said the old man with a smile. "The eldest son is in charge of hunting, the second eldest prepares the firewood, and the youngest grows vegetables and cooks at home. The dinner today had been made by my youngest

son."

At this time, the emperor's bodyguards arrived and respectfully waited for the emperor to depart. Judging by the appearance of the bodyguards, the man and his three sons recognized that the guest had been the emperor.

"Your family lives in peace on the mountain, which greatly pleases me." said the emperor with a smile. He then departed, and the man was paid with much silver.

A few days later, the emperor recalled the tasty corn porridge, and so had someone employ the youngest son to work in the imperial kitchen. His job was to cook corn porridge for the emperor and imperial families. From then on, corn porridge became one of the snacks listed on the imperial kitchen menu.

Notes: 1) folklore 民間傳説 2) bodyguard 護衛隊 3) spur 刺激 4) chase 追趕 5) porridge 粥 6) mushroom 蘑菇 7) hospitable 好客的 8) recognize 認出 9) menu 菜單

16 一品包子 Yipin Steamed Stuffed Buns

In Kaifeng（開封）, Henan Province, there is a snack called Yipin Steamed Stuffed Buns.This tasty bun has a thin skin and meat stuffing.Originally it was called "Taixue Steamed Bun（太學饅頭）" in the Song Dynasty. "Taixue" refers to an imperial college which was the highest institution of learning in ancient China.

During the early Northern Song Dynasty the Shenzong Emperor（神宗皇帝）made major efforts to enrich China and strengthen its military power.At the same time, the emperor encouraged talented students to apply for entry to study at the imperial college and allowed academically gifted students to start their official career soon after their graduation.

The emperor himself often visited the college to show his concern for students. One day upon visiting the college, the emperor asked the students to show him the food they ate. That day the college had served students with steamed buns so the emperor tasted them and then said, "I can only feel happy knowing that scholars eat this（以此養士，可無愧矣）." From that point on, the reputation of the college's steamed buns quickly spread. Whenever college students returned home to visit their parents, they always took the buns with them, wanting all their relatives and friends to eat the buns that had greatly satisfied the emperor. Over time people called the buns Taixue Steamed Bun.

During the Ming Dynasty Emperor Zhu Yuanzhang（朱元璋）chose his fifth son, Zhu Musu（朱木肅），to be a king. A king's position was equal to an official position of the first rank in the Ming government. "The first rank" means "yipin（一品）" in Chinese. King Zhu set up his residential palace in Kaifeng where he liked eating Taixue Steamed Buns and often entertained local nobles and officials with them. Thus local people renamed the same buns as Yipin Steamed Stuffed Buns.

Notes: 1) stuff 給……裝餡 2) bun 小圓麵包 3) stuffing 餡 4) enrich 使富裕；使豐富 5) academically 學術上

17 羊眼兒包子 Yangyanr Steamed Stuffed Buns

Yangyanr Steamed Stuffed Bun is a famous Hui cuisine dish（回民飲食）. "Yangyanr" means "sheep eyes（羊眼兒）." According to legend, one day Emperor Kangxi of the Qing Dynasty（康熙皇帝）put on common clothes and went out of his residential palace to taste Yangyanr Steamed Stuffed Buns. The emperor entered a food shop that sold Hui-styled steamed mutton buns. The shopkeeper served tea to the emperor, and said with a smile, "Your majesty, I'm afraid that you will be unhappy with the food I have to offer. In your residential palace you may

eat many delicacies, so how could you descend from your superior dignity into my humble shop just for Yangyanr Steamed Stuffed Buns? Honestly, I don't dare to present the buns to you."

The emperor was aware that the shopkeeper already knew his identity, but he behaved at ease, insisting that he would prefer eating Yangyanr Steamed Stuffed Buns.

"Your majesty," said the shopkeeper, "your presence in my humble shop is a great honor for me. Please wait a moment, and the buns will be ready soon."

A few minutes later, the shopkeeper returned with a plate of steaming hot buns whose smell greatly pleased the emperor. He grasped a bun with his chopsticks and put it into his mouth. To his surprise, the bun was delicious and had tasty ingredients.

"Where are the sheep eyes on the bun?" the emperor asked.

The shopkeeper replied, "Your majesty. The meat stuffing for the buns has no sheep's eyes at all. The buns each are small in size, and I do shape them like sheep's eyes, so people called them Yangyanr Steamed Stuffed Buns."

"Your buns really taste good. Please have them delivered regularly to my palace." said the emperor.

From then on, Yangyanr Steamed Stuffed Buns gained considerable fame across the city. As a result, other Hui people followed suit and made the same shaped buns. Gradually Yangyanr Steamed Stuffed Buns became one of the Hui people's favourite snacks.

Notes: 1) residential 居住的 2) superior 較高的 3) dignity 尊嚴 4) humble 謙遜的 5) honestly 如實地 6) ingredient（烹調的）原料 7) deliver 交付 8) considerable 相當多的

18 「狗不理」包子 Goubuli Steamed Stuffed Buns

Tourists who visit Tianjin（天津）can't miss the famous local snack called Goubuli Steamed Stuffed Buns.Made with half-fermented flour dough, each bun is shaped like chrysanthemum and contains juicy meat stuffing. More than 100 years ago, there was a peasant family named Gao（高）, and the father gave his son an infant name Gouzi（doggy，狗子）when he was born.

When Gouzi was 14 years old, his father had someone take him to Tianjin to begin an apprenticeship in a food shop to learn how to make steamed stuffed buns. Because he was clever, hardworking, and focused in preparing buns, Gouzi quickly became on expert at his trade.

After finishing his apprenticeship, Gouzi set up his own food shop to sell his buns. Due to his excellent skill, the reputation of Gouzi's buns grew daily as more and more customers went to his shop.

Gouzi was so busy making buns in his shop that he did not have time to talk to his customers. Thus some people made a joke, saying, "Gouzi sells buns and takes no notice of his customers." As days went by, people habitually called him Goubuli instead of Gouzi. Furthermore, they even named his buns as "Goubuli Buns," which literally means "Gouzi takes no notice of his customers." As "goubuli" refers to his buns, its meaning went even further suggesting, "Even dogs are not interested in steamed stuffed buns." Unexpectedly the unique name greatly promoted Gouzi's business.

As his goubuli business continued to expand, Gouzi decided to use a graceful trademark for his shop, rather than the nickname of goubuli, which sounded unpleasant. The new name was called "Dejuhao（德聚號），" which means "virtues gathering." In spite of the change, customers continued referring to Gouzi's buns as goubuli.

Governor Yuan Shikai（袁世凱）was greatly satisfied with goubuli Steamed Stuffed Buns. Once Governor Yuan went to the imperial palace, he presented the buns to Empress Dowager Cixi（慈禧太后）.The empress also thought they were delicious and had her servants take a special trip to Tianjing to purchase goubuli buns. The special purchase greatly enhanced the reputation of goubuli Steamed Stuffed Buns.

Notes: 1) ferment 發酵 2) dough 麵糰 3) chrysanthemum 菊花 4) juicy 多汁的 5) apprenticeship 學徒身份 6) nickname 綽號

19 餃子 Dumplings

Dumplings are a very traditional Chinese food. As dumplings evolved, they were given several different, including like laowan（牢丸）and bianshi（扁食）.

Northern Chinese people currently call dumplings jiaozi（餃子）, while Southern Chinese people prefer to call them huntun or won ton（餛飩）. Dumplings may be stuffed with a variety of food, such as pork, mutton, beef, and fish.

There are several stories concerning the origin of dumplings.According to one version, the dumpling was invented by Zhang Zhongjing（張仲景）, a well-known Eastern Han Dynasty herbal medical doctor who wrote the book Treatise on Febrile Diseases and Miscellaneous Diseases（《傷寒雜病論》）. This book first provided the theoretical basis for Chinese medicine, as well as the diagnostic and therapeutic principles based on an overall analysis of symptoms.

Once Zhang retired from his government affairs service and returned to his hometown, he found that in winter many local people had painful chilblain on the ear. Zhang realized that his clinic was so small that it couldn't accommodate the increasing number of chilblain patients, so he asked his brother to put up a tent in the village square and placed a cauldron in it. When the winter solstice arrived,

Zhang started offering medicinal herbs to chilblain patients.

His medicine was called quhan jiao'er tang（herbal soup to dispel the cold and protect the ears，祛寒嬌耳湯）. It consisted of mutton, red spicy peppers, and other necessary medicinal herbs. Zhang soaked them completely in water and heated them in the cauldron over a fire until the water boiled. Zhang then took all the things out of the cauldron, and minced them into stuffing. His assistants rolled out dough and made it into small pancakes. They put the stuffing on the centre of the pancakes and then wrapped them into the shape of an ear. These tiny things were named jiao'er（嬌耳）or "the ear protection" and were then all dropped into the herb soup to cook. Zhang offered each patient a bowl of the soup and two jia'er dumplings. The patients drank the soup and ate the dumplings and soon felt their whole body become warmer, including their ears.

For the following days, they continued eating dumplings and soup, and their ear chilblains gradually disappeared. Zhang kept offering the soup and jiao er dumplings until New Year's Eve. On the New Year's Day, local people all made dumplings as a symbol to celebrate New Year's Day and to rejoice over their recovery from the chilblains. This event turned into a tradition that has lasted until today.

Notes: 1) dumpling 餃子 2) a variety of 多種 3) treatise 專著 4) febrile 發熱的 5) miscellaneous 各種各樣的 6) theoretical 理論的 7) diagnostic 診斷 8) therapeutic 治療的 9) analysis 分析 10) symptom 症狀 11) chilblain 凍瘡 12) accommodate 給……提供食宿 13) cauldron 大鍋 14) celebrate 慶祝 16) rejoice 歡慶

20 窩窩頭 Steamed Corn Bread

Wowotou（steamed corn bread，窩窩頭）is made of corn flour or corn and bean flour. Steamed corn bread has a solid body and a round, flat base that

gradually becomes narrower toward the top. The centre of the base is curved inward, allowing steam to easily heat the bread.

There is an interesting anecdote about steamed corn bread. In 1900 a joint force of eight countries invaded China. Empress Dowager Cixi（慈禧太后）fled the capital to Xi'an with her palace attendants and staff before the foreign expeditionary force moved into Beijing.

On the way to Xi'an, the empress was hungry and extremely tired. The eunuchs searched everywhere, hoping to find food for the empress. They found nothing but one cold steamed corn bread from a villager nearby.

The empress quickly devoured the corn bread and then felt full. When she returned to her palace, she had cooks in the imperial kitchen make the steamed corn bread for her. The cooks made the bread in the same way the common people made it. However, the bread made in the imperial kitchen was small in size, consisting of refined corn, soybean flour, sugar, and sweet osmanthus petals.

The empress enjoyed eating the bread, so this kind of corn bread was later named xiao wowotou（small steamed corn bread，小窩窩頭）and became one of the best known snacks from the Qing Dynasty's imperial kitchens.

Notes: 1) corn flour 玉米麵 2) curve 成曲線 3) anecdote 逸事 4) osmanthus 桂花 5) petal 花瓣

21 饅頭 Steamed Buns

Chinese mantou（饅頭）traditionally refers to a steamed bun with or without fillings. In order to illustrate the difference, mantou generally implies "the steamed bun without fillings," and baozi（包子）"the steamed bun with fillings." Both steamed man tou and baozi are made with fermented flour.

The origin of the steamed bun can be traced back to the Three Kingdoms

Period. One story says that when Zhuge Liang（諸葛亮）served as the general commander of the Shu Kingdom（蜀國）, he was set to attack the kingdom of the Wei（魏國）in North China. However, he was worried that the minority armies might take this opportunity to harass the Shu Kingdom in Southwest China.Therefore Zhuge Liang wished to establish a good relationship with the minorities. Meng Huo（孟獲）was the top leader of the minorities and didn't accept Zhuge Liang's offerings of good-will. So Zhuge Liang went to the southwestern areas with his troops to fight against Meng Huo's army.

As Zhuge Liang and his troops crossed Lushui River（瀘水）, one of Zhuge's assistants proposed they behead some captives from Meng's troop and use their heads to offer a sacrificial ceremony to please the river deity. This purpose was to disperse the thick poisonous mist in the sparsely populated Lushui area, and clean away any poisonous elements in the river.

At that time, the derogatory term nanman（southern barbarians，南蠻）was applied to a wide range of southern non-Han people. Zhuge certainly did not agree to kill the nanman captives. Instead, he had his men slaughter oxen and sheep, grind up the meat and wrap it up with the dough parcels and shaped them like human heads. The soldiers followed Zhuge's instructions to steam these dough heads, which turned into a kind of sacrificial offerings with the name mantou（barbarian head，蠻頭）.

Zhuge brought the steamed mantou to the riverside where he placed it on an altar and then started the sacrificial ceremony. Afterwards he threw the mantou one after another into the river. After the ceremony, the mist disappeared, water became clean, and Zhuge's troops crossed the river without any difficulties.

This kind of bread was later introduced to Northern China. It was initially still called "mantou（barbarian head，蠻頭）." But since "man tou" did not sound like a good name for an everyday food, the ancient people renamed this bread

"mantou（steamed bun，饅頭）" in place of "蠻頭" because the Chinese character "蠻" was pronounced the same as "man（饅）." Gradually the steamed bun became a Northern Chinese staple food.

Notes: 1) minority 少數　2) harass 使煩惱；騷擾　3) sacrificial 獻祭的　4) ceremony 典禮　5) disperse 驅散　6) barbarian 野蠻的

22 油條　Deep-Fried Twisted Dough Sticks

"Deep-Fried Twisted Dough Stick" is a traditional breakfast snack. The origin of this snack is associated with Qin Hui（秦檜）, who served as prime minister during the reign of the Southern Song Dynasty Gaozong Emperor（高宗）.

In 1138 Gaozong designated Hangzhou as a "temporary capital," and signed a peace agreement with the Jin Kingdom（金國）in 1142. The previous year had seen the death of Yue Fei（岳飛）, one of China's most celebrated generals, who was also a hero in novels, stories and plays, because he had paid for his patriotism with his life. However, the groundless accusation against Yue Fei was a snare secretly set up by Qin Hui and his wife. After hearing of Yue Fei's death, common people in the capital were furious and really came to hate Qin Hui and his wife. Qin Hui came to be despised as the epitome of a traitor. Later, iron statues representing Qin Hui and his wife in chains were placed near Yue Fei's grave by the West Lake.

At that time there was an inn near where Yue Fei died that mainly sold oil-fried food. One day the inn boss was frying food when he heard of Yue Fei's death. The terrible news caused him to completely lose his temper, so he picked up a lump of flour dough from a basin and kneaded it into two small figures--a man and a woman. The boss pasted the two figures together back to back and dropped them into the oil pot while repeatedly shouting, "Go and drink boiled oil, Qin Hui!"

Upon hearing his shouting, people around understood what he was referring to. Soon people gathered around the pot and ate the figures while shouting and helping the boss knead more figures. Other inns and restaurants in the same city quickly followed suit, frying dough in the "Qin Hui" way. This practice spread far and wide across the country and has continued through dynasties until the present time.

Today, people prefer to call this food the "deep-fried twisted dough stick" （油條）rather than the oil-fried Qin Hui. However, in some areas, local people still keep using the old name Deep-fried Hui（油炸燴）or Deep-fried Ghost（油炸鬼）.

Notes: 1) temporary 暫時的　2) celebrate 慶祝　3) patriotism 愛國主義　4) groundless 無根據的　5) accusation 指控　6) snare 圈套　7) despise 鄙視　8) epitome 縮影　9) traitor 賣國賊　10) basin 盆 11) knead 揉成

23 元宵 Sweet Ball-Like Glutinous Rice Dumplings

Every Chinese household traditionally eats yuan-xiao（元宵）, sweet ball-like glutinous dumplings, on the fifteenth day of the first lunar month. The sweet balls symbolize family reunion, affection, and happiness, and are also known as tangyuan（湯圓, or balls in soup）.

Folklore tells how people started eating yuanxiao during the reign of the Han Dynasty Wu Emperor（漢武帝）. One snowy day Dongfang Shuo（東方朔）, a man of letters and one of the emperor's courtiers, went to the royal garden to pluck some blossoms for His Majesty. There he saw an imperial palace maid named Yuan Xiao（元宵）about to jump into a well to commit suicide. Dongfang rescued her, and it turned out that the maid had so desperately missed her family during festival occasions that she couldn't stand to live anymore. Dongfang, in great sympathy with her, thought of a way for her to see her family. He told her to wear a red dress and

go to the main street of the capital to read out a statement in the name of the Jade Emperor in Heaven: "I, the God of Fire, am here by order of the Jade Emperor to burn down Chang'an City. His Celestial Majesty will watch me perform my duty from the Southern Heavenly Gate up there."

The maid did what Dongfang told her. Those who heard her reading took her seriously and hastily asked for mercy. The girl in red replied, "Well, if you really want to avert this disaster, take this note to the emperor and let him think of a way out."

She gave them the note written on a red paper and left. The note was sent to the emperor, who opened it to find the following message: "Chang'an is doomed. The emperor's palace will be burnt down in a celestial fire on the sixteenth with red flames glowing at night."

Emperor Wu was stunned and asked Dongfang Shuo for advice. Dongfang said, "I heard that the God of Fire was fond of tangyuan (balls in soup) and that the maid Yuan Xiao was very good at making them. The God of Fire may also know that the tangyuan she makes is tasty. I would suggest that she make tangyuan on the evening of the fifteenth and Your Majesty burn incense and offer it to the God of Fire as a sacrifice. Your Majesty will also issue a decree ordering every family in the capital to make tangyuan for the God of Fire who will be pleased and change his mind. Your Majesty will also tell people in the capital to make lanterns and hang them on the main streets and back lanes, in the courtyards and on doors and display fireworks as if the whole city were ablaze on the night of the sixteen. The Jade Emperor will mistake this for the city on fire."

So Emperor Wu did as Dongfang proposed. Yuan Xiao and her family were reunited on that day. Since then Chinese people have taken Yuan Xiao Festival as an opportunity to get together with their families. Because the tangyuan made by the palace maid Yuan Xiao was the best, people now prefer to call it yuanxiao. Today, yuanxiao in China has many different flavours and is enjoyed by everybody.Preparing and eating yuanxiao during the Lantern Festival is a traditional delight.

Notes: 1) symbolize 象徵　2) courtier 朝臣　3) pluck採；摘　4) commit suicide 自殺　5) sympathy 同情　6) hastily 急速地　7) avert 避開　8) celestial 天空的　9) ablaze 著火

24 老婆餅　Wife Cake

"The Wife Cake" （老婆餅）originated in Chaozhou（潮州）, Guangdong Province. It is a baked cake with a golden yellow exterior and its filling consists of cotton paper thin flat layers that cover each other.

According to legend, towards the end of the Qing Dynasty, there was a teahouse in Guangzhou, which was well known for its different snacks and cakes. The teahouse bakery had a pastry master who was from Chaozhou. One day he returned home with varied teahouse-baked cakes.

After his wife had tried them all, the wife explained, "The pastry made in the teahouse is not as tasty as I expected. I think that the gourmet cake made by my parents is much better than any cakes you have offered."

Of course, the husband was not convinced by what his wife had said. He asked his wife to make a gourmet cake and let him taste it.His wife did it. Her cake appeared golden yellow with gourmet paste and sugar filling. The master baker ate it and couldn't help praising the gourmet cake for its sweet and delicious taste.

The next day the master baker took some gourmet cakes back to his teahouse and let his co-workers taste them. Even the teahouse boss joined in to praise his wife's cake. Finally he asked, "Which teahouse bakes such a wonderful cake?"

"This cake was done by my wife from Chaozhou!" responded the master baker.

"Well, it is the Chaozhou wife cake," said the boss.

Ever since then, the teahouse bakers started preparing this kind of cake to sell to customers. Thus the name "Wife Cake" gradually spread along with the popularity of the Chaozhou style cake.

Notes: 1) exterior 外部的 2) layer 層 3) tasty 可口的 4) gourmet 美食家；出自美食家之手的 5) popularity 流行

25 刀削麵 Knife-Sliced Noodles

"Knife-Sliced Noodles"（刀削麵）is a unique flavored, wheat-flour food enjoyed by local people in Shanxi Province. The knife used is really a curved and sharpened sheet specially made for this food. A noodle cook usually holds well-kneaded dough in his left palm as he grasps the knife between the fingers of his right hand, all the while facing a pot with boiling water. The cook then starts to horizontally slice the dough with his knife, and the sliced flakes leap into the pot. Each flake is about six inches long, triangular in shape but very thin. The flakes keep rolling up and down in the boiling water like silvery-colored fish frolicking in a rushing river. A skilled cook is able to slice as many as 200 dough flakes per minute.

The origin of knife-sliced noodles can be traced back to ancient times when Mongol horsemen occupied the Central Plains（中原）where the Han people lived.In order to prevent the Hans from rising up in rebellion, the Mongol soldiers confiscated all metal tools owned by each and every household.At the same time, they issued an order for every ten households to share only one kitchen knife for cooking.

One day, an old man was preparing noodles for lunch.He went out to fetch the shared knife to cut the well-kneaded dough into long thin noodle strips. The knife had been unexpectedly taken away by another family ahead of him. He had to return home and wait his turn.

On his way home, the old man saw a thin iron sheet lying on the ground. He picked it up and hid it under his clothes.

Upon arrival of home, the old man took out the iron sheet and said to himself, "Let's see if I can use this sheet in place of a knife." He kneaded the dough and sharpened the sheet.Afterwards he placed the dough in the palm of his left hand while picking up the sheet with his right hand.He started to horizontally slice the dough towards a pot with boiling water and the sliced flakes flew into the pot one after another. Soon the noodles were well done.

The old man scooped up the knife-sliced flakes from the pot, adding some sauce before he started eating. "Very good!" he thought. "This iron sheet is perfect. From now on, I won't need to line up again to wait for the shared kitchen knife."

Notes: 1) sharpen 磨快 2) dough 麵糰 3) horizontally 水平地 4) flake 小薄片 5) frolic 嬉戲 6) rebellion 造反 7) confiscate 沒收 8) household 家庭；戶 9) unexpectedly 出人意料地

26 過橋米線 Crossing-the-Bridge Rice Noodles

Guoqiao mixian or Guoqiao Rice Noodle（過橋米線）literally means "crossing-the-bridge rice noodle." This food is a local Yunnan rice noodle, which is made with a hot bowl of chicken broth, another bowl of rice noodles, vegetables, and several pieces of sliced raw fish, chicken, and ham. The broth usually remains boiling in the bowl for some time. Sliced raw ingredients and rice noodles are heated inside the bowl until they are edible.

There is a story that explains the origin of "Guoqiao Noodle." A long time

ago, according to the legend, there was a lake outside the town of Mengzi（蒙自）in the Yunnan area. There was a scenic island in the middle of the lake with green trees, beautiful pavilions, and tall towers. The island was a comfortable and appealing place for scholars to escape from the town and concentrate on studying classic books and poetry.

There was a scholar who stayed on the island to prepare for the imperial civil service exams. Every day, his wife delivered food to him by crossing over a wooden bridge to the island. However, the scholar often forgot to eat the food while it was warm because he was so deeply absorbed in his studies. His wife worried about this irregular diet would affect his health.

One day, his wife slaughtered a fat chicken and stewed it in a casserole. When it was well done, she offered it to her husband in a bowl of chicken broth in which she also added raw rice noodle and other ingredients. Over the surface of the soup was a layer of chicken fat in order to keep the soup from getting cold. Unexpectedly the rice noodles in the broth remained warm for some time and were still tasty. Her husband liked this style, so following that day, his wife continued to deliver the rice noodles cooked in the same way.

The scholar passed his civil service exams. Afterwards, he often recalled having been well treated by his wife who delivered rice noodles in chicken broth. The scholar therefore named the noodles "Crossing-the-bridge Rice Noodles" because his wife crossed the bridge to deliver his food every day.

This story about the scholar and his wife, and the new name of the rice noodles spread across the area, and many local people started cooking rice noodle in the same way as the scholar's wife did. As days went by, people continued refining the noodles'cooking methods, thus enabling it to spread far and wide in Yunnan Province.

Notes: 1) noodles 面條　2) broth 肉湯　3) edible 可食用的　4) pavilion 亭子

5) appealing 動人的　6) irregular 不規則的　7) stew 炖　8) casserole 沙鍋　9) refine 精煉；改進

27 皮蛋　Lime Preserved Eggs

What is the origin of the lime preserved egg? According to legend, during the Taichang period of the Ming Dynasty（明代泰昌年間）, there was a small teahouse in Wujiang County（吳江縣）, Jiangsu Province. Every day the tea house's proprietor was busy engaged serving customers who enjoyed drinking tea there. He usually poured the leftover brewed tea into the cinder.

The man raised several ducks in the teahouse yard, and these ducks liked laying eggs on the same ashes, so he collected eggs there. Sometimes he carelessly left out some eggs that were hidden inside the ashes.

One day, the proprietor unexpectedly found a few left-out eggs when he cleaned away the ashes mixed up with brewed tealeaves.He thought that these eggs couldn't be eaten because they had been covered by ash and brewed tealeaves for some time. He broke the shell of one of the eggs and saw something inside that appeared dark and glossy. After smelling the dark thing, he tasted it, and found it had a unique flavour.

Based on this accidental discovery, people continued to improve the process of making lime preserved eggs. Traditional Chinese medicine believes that the lime preserved egg has a cooling attribute that can help treat aching eyes, toothaches, high blood pressure, dizziness, and ringing ears.

People have currently developed a process to produce a preserved egg without lead. This process has pleased lime-preserved-egg eaters who now do not have to worry about the lead contamination.

Notes: 1) proprietor 業主　2) brew 沏（茶）　3) cinder 爐渣；煤渣　4) lime 石

灰　5) high blood pressure 高血壓　6) dizziness 頭暈　7) ringing ears 耳鳴　8) contamination 汙染

28 冰糖葫蘆　Candied Haws on a Bamboo Stick

The candied haws on a stick are both sour and sweet. Old and young people both enjoy eating this bright red dessert. The vendor typically uses a bamboo stick to pierce through the fruit one after another so that the haws remain in a row on the stick. Then the vendor coats each fruit with a thin layer of liquid candy to give it a lustrous sheen. Finally the vendor inserts each end of bunches of these haw sticks into a long thick rod and carries the rod to a farmers' fair or a traditional temple fair where the haw rod appears as a tree full of red fruit to passers-by.

There was a legend about the origins of candied haws. According to this legend, candied haws appeared during the reign of the Southern Song Dynasty Emperor Guangzong. The emperor's name is Zhao Ting（趙停）.

Zhao Ting had a concubine named Huang whom he loved very much.One day Lady Huang got sick and tired. She had eaten nothing for days. The imperial doctors treated her with a variety of valuable medicines, but she still did not recover. Emperor Zhao Ting worried all day long as his beloved concubine got worse. At his wit's end, he had someone put a notice seeking medical advice. An unknown herbal medicine doctor took off the note and went to the imperial residence where he diagnosed Lady Huang by feeling her wrist pulse. Afterwards he advised, "Boil red haws with crystal sugar and eat them before each meal, five to ten haws each time. In less than half a month, the sickness will disappear." In the beginning, nobody believed him, but Huang nonetheless ate the boiled candied haws in accordance with the doctor's advice.To everyone's surprise, Lady Huang quickly recovered and the emperor finally could relax.

Haws have some medical benefits such as relieving dyspepsia and aiding digestion. Perhaps Lady Huang's problem was that her daily diet consisted mainly of rich food that was difficult to digest. Perhaps the haws helped her digestion.

Later, knowledge of candied haws'medical benefits spread to the general population.The earliest way to sell candied haws was to string and sell them together. This gradually changed to the present method of putting candied haws on a bamboo stick.Although there is currently a variety of haw food on sale, common people still enjoy eating sour and sweet candied haws on a bamboo stick.

Notes: 1) candied 糖煮的 2) haw 山楂 3) vendor 小販 4) lustrous 有光澤的 5) sheen 光輝 6) concubine 妾 7) nonetheless 仍然；不過 8) dyspepsia 消化不良 9) digestion 消化

29 鱸魚 Perch

Perch is a very tasty fish. "The Later Ode to the Red Cliff（《後赤壁賦》）" one of ci poems（宋詞）by Su Dongpo（蘇東坡）of the Song Dynasty, describes the appearance of the perch. "At dusk today, I spread my fishing net and caught a fish. It has large lips and thin scales, which looks as if it were a Songjiang perch.（今者薄暮，舉網得魚，巨口細鱗，狀如松江之鱸）."

The following are two well-known perch stories.

The first story comes from The Romance of the Three Kingdoms（《三國演義》）.Once during winter Cao Cao（曹操）in Xuchang（許昌）held a large banquet to host his officials and officers. During the banquet one uninvited guest arrived.His name was Zuo Ci（左慈）.

When Zuo Ci saw only one fish course in the banquet, he said, "You should eat Songjiang perch when you have the fish course."

Cao Cao replied, "How could I get Songjiang perch in this area?"

"I can catch them with a fishing rod." Zuo replied. After saying that, he picked up a fishing rod and went to the pond nearby where he soon caught some perch.

"Well," said Cao Cao, "Is this perch really from the pond or did you bring them here with you?"

"Perch usually have two gills, but the songjiang perch has four gills. Please come and take a look if you doubt it."

Everyone came close up for a look. As expected, these perch each had four gills.

The second story occurred during the Jin Dynasty. There was an official named Zhang Han（張翰）, who served in a government office in Luoyang（洛陽）. One day in autumn while in a market, Zhang saw someone selling perch. The sight reminded him of the perch and water shields in his hometown. Thus he resigned his government post and returned to his hometown, saying that he longed for its local perch and water shields. Since then, "longing for water shields and perch（蓴鱸之思）" became synonymous with "homesickness."

Notes: 1) perch 鱸魚 2) lip 唇 3) scale 魚鱗 4) uninvited guest 不速之客 5) gill（魚）鰓 6) water shield 蓴菜 7) resign 辭職 8) long for 渴望 9) homesickness 思鄉病

30 鮑魚 Abalone

Baoyu（鮑魚）, and fuyu（鰒魚）both mean "abalone." There is a saying "鮑者包也，魚者余也" which literally means "the character bao（鮑）refers to another character bao（bag，包）; yu（魚）to another character yu（surplus，余）." Then "包余" indicates "there is always surplus of money in your bag."

Traditionally Chinese assume that the sea cucumber and shark's fin can strengthen masculine yang while the abalone and eatable bird's nest can strengthen the feminine yin. People usually present abalone to their relatives and friends as a lucky gift that also improves health.Moreover, on the New Year's Day or other festivals, abalone is seen as an auspicious dish on a dining table when hosting friends, relatives or important visitors.

Chinese people began eating abalone long time ago. According to Records of the Historian (《史記》) by Sima Qian (司馬遷), abalone was already regarded as a precious and delicious food. The Biography of Wang Mang in The Book of the Earlier Han Dynasty (《漢書王莽傳》) says, "Wang Mang's rebellion was to meet its doom soon.He was too worried to have meals and only drank wine and ate abalone livers (王莽事將敗，悉不下飯，唯飲酒，啖鮑魚肝)." However, in ancient times, only royal families and the upper classes could have an access to abalone, which was listed as one of the eight delicacies in both the Ming and Qing dynasties. Abalone was usually the first dish of full courses eaten by ancient high officials and noble lords.

In the Qing Dynasty, when high-ranking officials working along the coastal regions had an opportunity to go to the capital for an audience with the emperor, they would prepare gifts that included dried abalone. According to the ranking system, a first ranked official would offer pieces of abalone, each weighing 0.5 kilogram. Those of lower ranks would offer much smaller abalone according to their position.

Towards the end of the Republic of China (民國末年) there existed menus in Beijing called "Tan's Home Style Cuisine (譚家菜)," which included two well-known dishes: Braised Abalone in Soy Sauce (紅燒鮑魚) and Abalone in Oyster Sauce (蠔油鮑魚).

Fresh, dried or canned abalone is currently available in China. It is usually cooked in several ways--fried, steamed, braised, simmered, or grilled. Abalone tastes

best either steamed or stewed, although it can also be cooked and dressed with salad sauce.

Notes: 1) abalone 鮑魚 2) surplus 剩餘物 3) shark 鯊魚 4) masculine 陽性的 5) eatable 可食用的 6)feminine 陰性的 7) auspicious 吉兆的 8) rebellion 反叛 9) oyster 牡蠣 10) braise 以文火燉煮 11) simmer煨；燉

31 醋 Vinegar

The Chinese invented vinegar a long time ago. It is said that 3,500 years ago King Zhou, the last king of the Shang Dynasty（商朝紂王）, gouged the heart out of Bi Gan（比干）in an attempt to decoct it with other medicinal herbs to cure the sickness of his concubine Da Ji（妲己）. Bi Gan served as prime minister, and the appearance of his heart was said to be uniquely exquisite. In order to be effective, the medicinal decoction needed sorghum liquor. At that time, Shanxi's Fenjiu Liquor（汾酒）was a well-known alcoholic beverage. The king thus had workers in the Fenjiu workshop send the liquor to the Shang Dynasty capital.

The workers employed porters who would carry wine urns for the long distance journey up to the capital. Because the journey started in mid-summer, all the workers and porters suffered heat exhaustion. While sitting down by the road to rest, the workers opened the urns to see if the liquor still tasted good. Unexpectedly the liquor in the urns had turned sour. The workers and porters were alarmed since they knew that they would be beheaded for presenting the sour wine to the king in the capital.In a state of despair, they decided to commit suicide by drinking all the sour wine. Two hours later, they were still alive, their heat exhaustion disappeared and they all felt refreshed from the journey. Instead of continuing their trip to the capital, they fled back home in the countryside where they distilled more sour wine.At that time, it was discovered that vinegar could be used to treat anything from diarrhoea to the common cold.

Generally speaking, northern style vinegar is usually produced with Chinese sorghum, barley, pea, millet or corn, while southern style vinegar contains only rice or bran. Northern Chinese like Lao Chencu（Age-Old Vinegar，老陳醋）from Shanxi Province, where Qingxu County（清徐縣）is considered the best place to distil high-quality vinegar because of the excellent local water source. However, southern Chinese usually prefer drinking Xiangcu（Aromatic Vinegar，香醋）produced in Zhenjiang City（鎮江）, which was an ancient rice market. Later, the Qing Dynasty central government accepted Li Hongzhang's（李鴻章）suggestion to move the market to Wuhu（蕪湖）. Located south of the Changjiang River, Zhenjiang is known for the high-quality of rice grown around the city. Traditionally rice is an important raw material for vinegar production: the better rice, the better the vinegar.

The phrase "chicu（drinking vinegar，吃醋）" is synonymous with "jealousy," but most people do not know why there is this connection. During the Tang Dynasty Emperor Li Shimin（李世民）once decided to offer some beautiful ladies to one of his ministers named Fang Xuanling（房玄齡）. Fang's wife heard of this offer, and she resolutely refused the emperor's offer. The emperor called Fang's wife in and said, "If you lose your jealousy of your husband, you will continue to live in peace, otherwise you have to drink the poisonous wine and die."

Upon hearing the emperor's words, she drank the poisonous wine in one gulp. It turned out the cup was actually filled with vinegar instead of poisonous wine. Although the emperor stopped presenting beautiful ladies to Fang Xuanling, this story spread far and wide, and people began to use "chicu" to imply "jealousy of a lover."

Notes: 1) invent 發明　2) vinegar 醋　3) decoct 熬；煎（藥等）4) appearance 外表　5) decoction 煎；煮　6) porter 搬運工人　7) exhaustion 精疲力竭　8)

behead 把……斬首　9) diarrhoea 腹瀉　10) barley 大麥　11) millet 小米　12) aromatic 芳香的　13) resolutely 堅決地　14) poisonous 有毒的　15) gulp 吞嚥

32 辣椒　Spicy Pepper

Red pepper originally came from Mexico, Central America, the West Indies, and parts of South America where it is called capsicum pepper. The Spanish found it in the New World and brought it back to Europe. Before the arrival of Spaniards, Indians in Peru and Guatemala used capsicum pepper to treat stomach pains and other ailments. It was introduced into China around the end of the 17th century. Local people in Chaozhou area, Guangdong Province, call red pepper fanjiao（番椒）, which means "foreign pepper."

While it is not clear how exactly the red pepper was introduced into China, several stories exist regarding this matter. The pepper could have been brought along China's Ancient Northwestern Silk Route（西北絲綢之路）, through Zheng He's Voyages to Western Oceans（鄭和下西洋）, or even into Guangdong and Guangxi by way of coastal trade routes. According to the latest research, red pepper might have been first introduced to Jiangsu, Zhejiang, Guangdong and Guangxi provinces. Gradually it spread to Guizhou, Hunan, Sichuan, and then to other places in China.

Red pepper was first used for ornamental purposes rather than for eating, but during the early Qing Dynasty, local people in Guizhou and its neighbouring areas began to eat pepper. During the period of Emperor Kang Xi's reign, people there used the pepper to replace salt, which was then in short supply in Guizhou.

Down to the period of Emperor Jiaqing's reign（嘉慶年間）, pepper was not eaten in Hunan. However, towards the end of the Qing Dynasty, pepper became quite popular among local people there. The historical record shows that at that time local people usually disliked eating their meals if dishes contained no pepper, and even added spicy pepper to some of their soups.

Based on written historic books, the reign of Emperor Jiaqing might be the earliest time that some local peasants from Sichuan started growing and eating red pepper. Gradually the red pepper grew everywhere in western Sichuan as a common vegetable. People usually called the pepper "haijiao（sea pepper，海椒）" indicating that it came from overseas countries.

Towards the end of the Qing Dynasty peasants grew red pepper everywhere across Sichuan and restaurants used it to make spicy dishes. Peppers currently grow all year around in Chengdu.Vegetable markets usually provide green hot pepper in May, red hot pepper in June, and large-sized red pepper in lantern shape both in June and July. Local Sichuan Province cuisine is known for being hot and spicy, but such dishes nonetheless account for less than thirty percent of all of Sichuan's dishes.

Notes: 1) capsicum 辣椒　2) Spaniard 西班牙人　3) stomach 胃　4) ornamental 裝飾的　5) spicy 辣的

33 蘿蔔　Turnip

Turnips are sweet, crispy, and juicy. Since ancient times, there have been many interesting stories regarding about turnips.

During the Three Kingdoms Period, Liu Bei（劉備）and Sun Quan（孫權）'s united forces defeated Cao Cao（曹操）and his troops at the Battle of the Red Cliff（赤壁）. Soon after the battle, Cao Cao and his soldiers fought their way out along Huarong Pass（華容道）. Because of the hot weather, hunger, and thirst, the soldiers couldn't walk any further.At that time, they happened to pass by an extensive turnip plot. The soldiers quickly crowded into the field where they pulled

up turnips to appease their hunger. Later, the field became known as "Rescuing Cao's Troops' Field（救曹田）."

More than 1300 years ago, under the rule of Wu Zetian（武則天）, ancient China's only female emperor, the country was generally peaceful.

Once in autumn, close to the Eastern Gate of Luoyang（洛陽）, there was a vegetable plot where a one-meter-long turnip grew. The turnip's upper part appeared green and the lower part white. Local peasants presented the vegetable as a miracle to the imperial palace.

This enormous turnip really pleased the female emperor when it was on display in the palace. She ordered imperial cooks to make dishes using the turnip. Although the cooks knew that it was almost impossible to produce a tasty turnip dish, they didn't give up, and instead worked hard in an attempt to find a way to satisfy the female emperor. They shredded the turnip and mixed it with other delicacies from land and sea. Then the cook stewed the ingredients until they were well done.

After the female emperor ate the stewed turnip and drank the broth, she named the dish "Almost Nest of Cliff Swallows（假燕窩）" because this food tasted unique and its flavour was like the dish Eatable Nest of Cliff Swallows.

From then on, princes, dukes, ministers, and noble families started using turnips as a main ingredient in dishes prepared for banquets or dinners for guests.

Notes: 1) crispy 清脆的　2) juicy 多汁的　3) extensive 廣大的　4) rescue 挽救　5) miracle 奇蹟　6) swallow 燕子

34 譚家菜　Tan's Home-Style Cuisine

Tan's Home-Style Cuisine（譚家菜）has existed for more than one hundred years and originally came from Tan Zonghou（譚宗後）'s family.

Tan Zonghou loved delicacies and tasty food all his life. When he was an official in a government department during the late Qing Dynasty in Beijing, he and his colleagues often took turns entertaining each other with banquets. When it was Tan's turn, he invited his colleagues to eat at home, and he personally took care of every single matter related to the dinner's arrangement. Gradually Tan's home style cuisine gained a reputation among officials in Beijing. Later, due to his official career frustration, Tan had to depart Beijing and return home.

During the reign of the Qing Dynasty Xuantong Emperor（宣統年間，1909—1911）, Tan Zonghou's son Tan Qing（譚青）, came to Beijing. After the Republic of China（民國）was founded, Tan Qing served as a secretary for a government department, and he often accompanied higher officials to dinner or banquets. Apart from this, Tan Qing enjoyed making friends and also loved delicacies and tasty food.Like his father, he entertained distinguished guests with dinner banquets at home on a regular basis, thus promoting the development of Tan's home style cuisine.Unfortunately, his family's financial situation deteriorated, so Tan Qing had to use his family style cuisine to start a business in order to help his family make ends meet.Gradually the Tan's family style cooking became one of China's best known family style cuisines.

Traditionally customers had to go to Tan's home if they wanted to eat his home style food, but the Tan family members would not stand outside to greet them.After customers have drunk wine through three rounds, a service person would begin to place dishes on the table.Usually the first dish is Braised Shark's Fin in Brown Sauce（黃燜魚翅）, the second Nest of Cliff Swallows in Light Soup（清湯燕菜）, and the third is abalone（鮑魚）. Many other dishes are offered after these courses, the final one of which is sweet and salty pastries. When the Tan's home style feast is over, everybody stands up and walks into a reception room where they eat fruit and drink tea.

Notes: 1) delicacy 精美的食品；美味佳餚 2) colleague 同事 3) frustration 挫折 4) financial 財政的 5) deteriorate 惡化 6) make ends meet 使收支相抵

35 四菜一湯 Four Dishes and a Soup

According to legend, in the early Ming Dynasty after Zhu Yuanzhang（朱元璋）came to the throne, a series of natural disasters led to crop failures all across China, plunging most common people into extreme poverty. High officials and noble families, however, continued to enjoy a luxurious life.

One day, when it was the empress's birthday, government ministers and officials attended her birthday celebration.

When everyone was seated at tables, with each table seating ten guests, Emperor Zhu asked for the food courses to start. The first course was Stir-fried Radish; the second was stir-fried Leeks; the third and fourth were two large bowls of green vegetables, and the final course was a bowl of tofu soup with chopped green onions.

Emperor Zhu entertained guests with plain food, thus suggesting that all the guests should live frugal lives. After the dinner the emperor announced a rule in front of the visitors, "From now on, courses for any banquet are no more than four dishes and one bowl of soup. The empress's birthday banquet has set a good example. Those who violate the rule will be severely punished without mercy."

In the mid and late Qing Dynasty, prices rose and people tended to seek a luxurious life. Some insightful men at that time proposed entertaining guests at a banquet with Four Dishes and a Bowl of Soup. The Qing-styled Four Dishes usually contained two meat dishes and two vegetable ones.

In 1950, after the founding of the People's Republic of China, Zhou Enlai（周恩來）, the first premier of the State Council, stipulated that the Four Dishes and a

Bowl of Soup should be served to host participants for government meetings and conferences. These dishes and soups were all common home style meat and vegetables.

Notes: 1) luxurious 奢侈的 2) radish 蘿蔔 3) leek 韭 4) frugal 節儉的 5) insightful 有見地的

36 大排檔 Sidewalk Snack Booths

The phrase paidang (sidewalk snack booths，排檔) can be traced back to a corrupt ancient practice. According to the Southern Song Dynasty imperial menu, the imperial family members did not have meat dishes every day. Instead palace service officials often used their own money to invite the emperor, nobles, and ministers to dinner. Paidang（排當）refers to the way these palace service officials took turns offering these meals.

In the beginning, palace officials paid the bills by themselves. Some even looked for a way to be reimbursed. Down to Emperor Lizong's reign of the same dynasty（宋理宗）, palace officials had access to the imperial central government and local financial offices for their bills'reimbursement. During that period, Chen Zongli（陳宗禮）, a local military commander in Guangdong, was transferred to work as a senior assistant in the General Military Headquarters（樞密院）in the capital where he witnessed this "corruption".

He saw that people of lower rank invited those of higher ranks to dinner only for the purpose of reaping some profit from their bills' reimbursement or seeking special favour or help. So Chen thus submitted a written report to the concerned department in order to prohibit paidang. However, Chen got no response, and pai dang continued to be practiced.

Later, the phrase "paidang" came into common use, referring to a small

open-air, street-side food business. Each place has simple facilities, like a number of tables and chairs, and provides inexpensive food to meet the demands of common people. Local people in Guangdong call this kind of space dang（檔）Pai（排）traditionally refers to "line up," indicating that the dangs stand in line along the street. Gradually the union of both pai and dang implies street-side snack booths.

Notes: 1) reimburse 償還；報銷 2) commander 指揮員 3) headquarters 總部 4) phenomenon 現象 5) prohibit 禁止

37 皇帝進膳制度 Dining Arrangements for an Emperor

In ancient China, imperial cooks who served kings or emperors had official rank and received the same salary as other officials in similar positions. During the Qin and Han dynasties, a person who led the imperial cooks was called taiguan ling（太官令）, which literally means "senior official." Tai guan remained the name of a house where imperial meals were cooked and prepared until the Northern Qi State（北齊，550-577 AD）, when taiguan was replaced by guang lu si（光祿寺）, until the end of the Qing Dynasty.

In accordance with Rites of the Zhou Dynasty（《周禮》）, musicians would play music while the king ate his meal. In later dynasties, although musicians seldom played music during the king or emperor's daily meals, some other rules were added to further demonstrate the king or emperor's dignity. For example, no one was allowed to dine with the emperor without his explicit permission.In ancient China the king or emperor was the supreme ruler in the country. If he invited someone to dinner, it was usually considered as a significant favor bestowed upon participants. Qingke chifan（invite someone to dinner，請客吃飯）is a common expression in modern Chinese, but cifan（grant someone a meal，賜飯）or shangchi（award someone with food，賞吃）more accurately displays the status between the emperor and his subjects in ancient China.

In the Qing Dynasty, before preparing the emperor's meal, the cooking staff had to submit a list of food, soup, and dishes to be approved by the minister of the internal affairs. The imperial kitchen prepared the emperor's meals; the imperial tea house supplied varied tea, and made milk tea with tea, cream, and salt; the imperial bakery produced pastries and cakes.

At the start of a meal, the emperor might have his bodyguard give notice to the imperial cooking house. An official who was in charge of the imperial cuisine immediately arranged for the eunuchs to lay on a table a number of big and small covered bowls filled with a variety of foods and soup. The emperor would not start to eat even after everything was ready.Instead he would watch small silver sticks that were inserted in the food. The change of the metal colour might indicate that the food was poisoned. After the silver metal test, a eunuch had to "taste" to further guarantee that the food was not poisoned. This process was called "food tasting（嘗膳）."

In the Qing Dynasty, the emperor usually had two meals a day. His first meal started at six o'clock and ended at eight in the morning; his second meal was between two and four o'clock in the afternoon. Each meal usually contained 15 to 25 kinds of food in a number of big and small exquisite bowls and other utensils. The Dowager Empress Cixi（慈禧太后）preferred rich food.Each time her cooks provided her with over 100 varied foods, including 10 pork dishes and other dishes made of chicken, duck, or mutton. Before her meal, Empress Dowager Cixi usually preferred eating fruit and drinking tea. In order to please the empress, cooks racked their brains, shaping some of dishes into beautiful patterns like a phoenix, butterfly, flowers, or even Chinese characters like fu（福, happiness）or shou（壽, Longevity）.Emperor Kangxi（康熙）was different, preferring simple over elaborate meals.He had no special requirements for food.

When the emperor's meal was over, he usually offered his leftover dishes or

food to his subjects, including concubines, children, or ministers.In ancient society being offered the emperor's leftover food was considered to be a great honour.

Notes: 1）similar 相似的　2）musician 音樂家　3）demonstrate 證明　4）significant 重要的　5）bestow upon 把……贈與　6）status 地位　7）bakery 麵包房　8）eunuch 太監　9）phoenix 鳳凰　10）butterfly 蝴蝶　11）requirement 要求

茶典故與趣談 Interesting Stories About Chinese Tea

1 龍井茶 Longjing Tea

According to legend, during Emperor Qianlong's（乾隆皇帝）inspection tour in South China, he came to the foot of Shifeng Hill（獅峰山）in Hangzhou where he watched local women picking tea leaves. On the spur of the moment, he decided to help them pick tealeaves. Just as he had collected a handful of leaves, a eunuch arrived and said, "The dowager empress is sick.Please return to the capital as soon as possible."

Upon hearing of his mother's sickness, the emperor immediately put his collection of leaves into his pocket, and departed for the capital.It turned out that the empress dowager only had an upset stomach from eating too much food. When the empress dowager saw her son arrive, she smelt something fragrant and refreshing coming from the emperor.

"What good things did you bring?" asked his mother.

The emperor had no idea where the fragrance came from. He instinctively touched his pocket and realized that the fragrance came from the tealeaves that he picked at the foot of the hill in Hangzhou. These leaves became dry in his pocket while the emperor travelled from Hangzhou to the capital.

A court maid used the leaves to brew up tea and presented it to the empress dowager. As expected, the tea water released a faint scent. The empress dowager

drank the tea, and soon afterwards, her stomachache was over.

The emperor's mother said cheerfully, "Longjing tea from Hangzhou is miraculous."

The emperor was happy as he saw a smile grow on his mother's face. He thus issued an order to designate the eighteen Longjing tea plants located in front of the Hugong Temple（胡公廟）at the foot of Shifeng Hill as imperial tea plants. The emperor's order also proclaimed that each year fresh tea picked from the imperial tea plants should be given to the dowager empress.

Notes: 1) on the spur of the moment 隨興所至 2) dowager 貴婦 3) refreshing 提神的 4) instinctively（出於）本能地 5) miraculous 神奇的 6) designate 指派

2 黃山毛峰 Huangshan Maofeng Tea

Mt.Huangshan is a famous tourist attraction in Anhui Province. Huangshan Maofeng Tea（黃山毛峰）grows on the mountain, and there is a legendary story behind this tea.

One day during the Ming Dynasty Xizong Emperor's reign（明熹宗天啟年間，1605－1627）, Xiong Kaiyuan（熊開元）, a newly appointed magistrate of Yi County（黟縣）, hiked Mt.Huangshan for a spring excursion. On his way, he came across an old Buddhist monk who carried a bamboo basket in his arms. The monk let him stay overnight in a monastery where the abbot brewed tea to host him. Covered with a white fluffy substance, the tea leaves had a light yellow color and were shaped like a sparrow's tongue. As the abbot poured hot boiled water into the tea bowl, the steam immediately encircled the rim of the bowl, rushed forward to the bowl's centre, and then rose above half a meter high. The steam continued to make a circle in the air before turning into a white lotus flower. The flower kept rising, turning into a big cloud of mist that gradually drifted away in fragrant wisps.

The abbot told Xiong that the name of the tea was Huangshan Maofeng.The next day when Xiong departed the monastery, the abbot presented him with a small package of tea and a gourd filled with spring water from the mountain. The abbot said that the sight of the white lotus flower would emerge if this spring water were used to brew the tea.

Xiong returned to his office in Yi County. Once the magistrate of Taiping County（太平縣）visited him. Xiong hosted him and brewed Huangshan Maofeng Tea.The sight of the white lotus flower emerging again really amazed his visitor. The Taiping magistrate later went to the capital. He expected to present the unique tea to the emperor in exchange for a handsome reward.

The magistrate had an audience with the emperor, who asked him to display the wonderful tea on spot. However, the unique sight did not emerge no matter what he did with the tea. At last, the magistrate confessed that he was unfaithful to the emperor and said that the tea belonged to Xiong Kaiyuan, the magistrate of Yi County. The emperor immediately had Xiong be presented at the palace court to explain why the tea failed to present the lotus flower.

Upon arrival at the palace court, Xiong discovered that the failure to present the miraculous image of the lotus flower was due to the fact that he had used common water rather than the spring water from Mt.Huangshan. So Xiong went back to Mt.Huangshan where he revisited the abbot for the water.

When he returned to the palace court, Xiong used the spring water to brew the tea in a jade cup, and the expected miracle occurred. The sight of lotus flower brought the emperor joy, and he said to Xiong, "You have rendered great service by offering the unique tea. So I have decided to promote you to governor of the areas south of the lower reaches of the Yangtze River."

Xiong was overcome with gratitude, but soon resigned his commission and became a Buddhist monk in the monastery on Mt.Huangshan.

Notes: 1) legendary 傳說的 2) magistrate 地方行政官 3) excursion 短途旅行 4) abbot 住持 5) fluffy 絨毛（狀）的 6) substance 物質 7) wisp（煙等的）一縷 8) amaze 使大為驚奇 9) unfaithful 不忠誠的

3 鐵觀音 Tieguanyin Tea

Tieguanyin Tea is grown in Anxi County（安溪）, Fujian Province. In Naxi County there is a folk story about the origin of the tea.According to legend, during the reign of the Qing Dynasty Qianlong Emperor（乾隆皇帝）, there was a local tea grower named Wei（魏）. He was good at making tea, and every early in the morning and late in the evening he would produce three cups of tea to enshrine the Goddess of Mercy（觀音菩薩）.

One night, Wei had a dream in which he saw a tea plant on a high cliff.In the dream, he extended his hands, hopping to pick tea leaves, but the sound of barking dogs woke him up from the dream. The next day, Wei found a tea plant on a cliff, which appeared exactly like the one from his dream. He then picked some tea leaves and brought them home to be carefully processed. After he tasted the newly processed tea, he believed that this tea was the king of all teas because of its unique taste.

Wei returned to the cliff. He dug out the plant and re-grew it inside his courtyard. A few years later, the tea plant turned to be a large tree with strong branches and densely-covered leaves. It is said that local people there pronounced the word "cha（tea，茶）" as "tie（iron，鐵）" and that they had the new tea only because of Guanyin, the Goddess of Mercy, who appeared in Wei's dream. The tea plant was thus named "tie-guanyin". Since then Tieguanyin Tea began to be known throughout China.

Notes: enshrine 把……奉為神聖

4 大紅袍 Dahongpao Tea

Dahongpao Tea is a kind of Oolong Tea that grows on Wuyi Mountain（武夷山）, Fujian Province. A long time ago, according to legend, a scholar passed through Wuyi Mountain on his way to the capital where he would take the imperial exams. As he travelled along the mountainous path, he got sick and fell down. The abbot from Tianxin Buddhist Monastery（天心廟）found the scholar and brewed him some tea to drink. The scholar quickly got well and continued his trip to the capital where he passed his exams as the Number One Scholar.

One spring the scholar returned to Wuyi Mountain to express his sincere thanks to the abbot for the great favour done for him. The abbot accompanied the scholar to a high cliff. Three tea plants with strong branches that were densely covered with leaves were growing on the side of the cliff. Under the sunshine, clusters of flourishing tea leaf buds all had a purple-red colour.

The abbot explained, "Last year, you recovered from the sickness after drinking the tea water brewed with leaves from these plants. A long time ago, when the tea leaves from these plants sprouted in spring, local tea collectors would beat drums to assemble monkeys. Upon the sound of the drums, all the monkeys would arrive, put on red-coloured jackets and pants, and climb the cliff to pick tealeaves for the collectors. Afterwards the collectors processed the leaves until they were well done.These processed leaves can cure diseases."

Upon hearing of the story, the scholar expressed a desire to present these leaves to the emperor. So the next day, all the monks gathered at the foot of the cliff. They started a religious service, burning incense and shouting together, "Tealeaves are budding!" After the service, they climbed the cliff to pick leaves, which were then carefully processed and packaged in a tin box.

The scholar took the tea box to the capital.Upon arriving there, he was told

127

that that the empress lay in bed because of her stomach trouble. The scholar brewed tea with the leaves from the mountain and let the empress drink it. As expected, her stomach trouble soon disappeared.

The unique tea brought the emperor great joy. He sent the scholar a bright red robe, asking him to take it to the mountain. The scholar went back once again to the mountain where he climbed the cliff and reached the plants.He unfolded the robe at the foot of the plants, hoping to cover them; the buds on the trees glittered in the sunshine.People nearby believed that the bright red robe dyed the bud leaves red.

Later, people called these plants "dahongpao", which means "the bright red robe". Since then, every year Dahongpao Tea became a regular tribute tea to the imperial families in the capital.

Notes: 1) number one scholar 狀元 2) cluster（花等的）束；簇 3) purple-red 紫紅色 4) assemble 聚集 5) glitter 閃爍

5 君山銀針 Junshan Yinzhen Tea

Junshan Yinzhen Tea（君山銀針）grows in Junshan（君山）, Hunan Province, where it is said that the first seed sowed can be traced back 4,000 years ago.

According to legend, during the Late Tang Dynasty（後唐，923—936）, after Li Siyuan（李嗣源）ascended the throne, he went to the palace court for the first time to sit upon his throne.His attendant placed a cup before the Emperor with some tea leaves inside. While the attendant poured hot boiled water into the cup, a mass of steam rose up filling the air. Out of this steam gradually emerged a white crane that nodded three times to the emperor before the crane flew towards the sky.

The emperor looked back at the cup. All the tea leaves were standing upright in the water like a group of bamboo shoots breaking ground in the spring. A moment later, the tea leaves slowly sank like snow flakes falling on the ground. All this amazed the emperor, and so he asked the attendant how a cup of tea could produce such a miracle.

"This is due to baihe quan（白鶴泉，white crane spring water）in Junshan used for brewing Yinzhen Tea（銀針茶）." the attendant replied.

The emperor was so happy to hear this explanation that he immediately designated Yinzhen Tea as the imperial tribute tea.

6 白毫銀針 Baihao Yinzhen Tea

This tea grows in Zhenghe County（政和縣）, Fujian Province.People call this tea Baihao Yinzhen Tea（白毫銀針）because the tea leaves are covered with a white fluffy substance and look like silvery needles. Its name literally means "white hair silvery needle."

A long time ago, according to legend, the Zhenghe region suffered a severe drought, and epidemics plagued the local population. At that time, local people believed that only the juice of celestial grass could eliminate the epidemics. Therefore, many young men went to Donggong Mountain（洞宮山）to search for the celestial grass that grew near the Dragon Well（龍井）. Unfortunately, no one returned home from this journey.

There was a family with two brothers and one sister. The three of them decided to take turns going to the mountain to look for the celestial grass. The eldest brother went first. When he arrived at the foot of the mountain, he came across an old man, who advised him by saying, "If you turn around while hiking the mountain, you will not find the grass."

The brother continued his journey and soon started to hike the mountain.About halfway up, he stopped for a break.There he found nothing around but stones and rocks.At this very moment, a loud shout burst out. He turned round and was

immediately turned to stone.

The young brother was the second to go to the mountain. Like his eldest brother, he was turned to stone because he too turned around at the half waypoint up the mountain.

So the difficult task fell on the sister, who went last.On the way up the mountain, she came across the same old man who offered her the same advice. The man also gave her a roasted glutinous rice cake.

The sister continued to hike after leaving the old man. When she reached the place where her two brothers turned into stones, a strange sound suddenly burst out in all directions. The sister immediately clogged her ears with the glutinous cake and resolutely refused to turn round. She kept hiking until she reached the Dragon Well, where she picked the blades of the grass, and at the same time she watered the grass with water from the well.Gradually the celestial grass blossomed and yielded many grass seeds. The sister collected the seeds and returned home where she sowed the seeds all over the hillsides. Her sowing may be the origin of Baihao Yinzhen Tea.

Notes: 1) silvery 銀色的 2) epidemic 流行病 3) plague 瘟疫；使染瘟疫 4) burst out 突然……起來 5) roast 烤 6) hillside 山腰

7 白牡丹 Baimudan Tea

Baimudan Tea grows in Fuding County（福鼎縣）, Fujian Province.Baimudan literally means "white peony."

According to legend, during the Western Han Dynasty there was a prefecture chief named Mao Yi（毛義）, who resigned his position and followed his mother into the remote mountains.

One day, Mao and his mother arrived at a green hill where they smelled a unique fragrance. An old man told them that the fragrance came from the 18 white peony plants alongside a lotus flower pond. The two thus decided to live close to this beautiful place.

One day, Mao's mother became sick with her fatigue and age. Mao looked everywhere for medicinal herbs. One night, Mao had a dream in which an aged celestial being said to him, "Carps and fresh tea are key to the recovery of your mother's health."

It was a severe winter, and the cold weather froze the pond over. However, encouraged by the celestial instruction, Mao went to the pond where he broke ice and jumped into chilly-cold water to catch carps.

After catching enough carps, as he wondered where to pick fresh tealeaves, something miraculous happened. These 18 peony plants unexpectedly turned into the 18 celestial tea plants, each being covered with many fresh leaves. Mao picked these leaves and dried them. He stewed the carps with the fresh tea leaves, and as expected, his mother recovered after eating the newly prepared medicinal food.

Later, people named this tea "Baimudan Tea (white peony tea)" because the leaves were covered with white fluffy substance and shaped like a white peony.

Notes: 1) peony 牡丹 2) chilly-cold 寒冷的 3) miraculous 奇蹟般的

8 茉莉花 Jasmine Tea

A long time ago, there was a tea trader whose name was Chen Guqiu（陳古秋）. One day, he had a chat with a tea master who was good at judging the taste and quality of different tea. Their ongoing chat reminded him of a tea package given to him by a girl from South China. Chen took it out and invited the master to taste it.

As Chen opened the cup-lid and poured hot boiling water into the cup, they

first smelt the fragrance from the tea and then saw a beautiful girl rise from the steam. She was holding a bunch of jasmine flowers in her hands and then disappeared a moment later.

Chen looked puzzled.

"This tea belongs to a category of superb teas," explained the master. "It is called Bao'en Tea（報恩茶）." Bao'en literally means "pay a debt of gratitude".

Chen recalled his memory of an earlier encounter with the helpless girl in an inn as he was in South China for business. The girl told him that her father had died, and she had no money to pay the funeral service for her father. Chen sympathized with the girl's sad situation and gave her some money.

Three years later, Chen went to the south again where he stayed in the same inn. The inn owner passed to him a small package of tea, saying, "Three years ago, a girl asked me to hand over this package to you."

"Why does she only hold jasmine flowers?"

Chen and the master dropped some of the tea into another cup, and once again they poured into the cup hot boiled water. The girl reappeared in the steam, holding a bunch of jasmine flowers.

Chen tasted the tea and said, "It suggests, I believe, that jasmine flowers can be added to tea."

From then on, a kind of new tea was on sale at tea markets named Jasmine Tea.

Notes: 1) a bunch of 一束 2) encounter 遇到 3) helpless 無助的

9 碧螺春 Biluochun Tea

Biluochun Tea grows in Jiangsu Province's Dongting region.According to legend, long ago there was a girl who lived on Dongting Lake's（洞庭湖）Western Hill. Her name was Biluo（碧螺）. On Dongting Lake's Eastern Hill lived a young man named Axiang（阿祥）. These two were in love with each other.

One year a dragon emerged in Tai Lake（太湖）. He was ferocious and evil and attempted to use force to marry Biluo. Axiang was determined to fight the evil dragon.

One evening, Axiang grasped a fishing fork and went to the Western Hill where he and the dragon fought for seven days and nights. Both sides were completely exhausted, and Axiang fell down unconscious. Biluo carefully looked after Axiang as his injuries got worse day by day.

One day, Biluo went out, looking for medicinal herbs. She came to the place where Axiang and the dragon fought. There she saw a small tea plant that grew very well. She thought that she should take good care of the plant because it had witnessed the fight between Axiang and the dragon.

During the Qingming Festival（清明節）in early April bud leaves sprang out all over the plant. Biluo picked some bud leaves and brewed them at home. She let Axiang drink this tea water. Miraculously, Axiang slowly recovered after drinking the new tea.

Just as the two young people expected a happy life together, Biluo succumbed to poor health, fell into Axiang's arms and died.Terribly saddened by her sudden death, Axiang buried Biluo by the tea plant. From then on, he worked hard to grow more tea plants and produce good tea.In order to honour Biluo, Axiang named his tea "Biluochun Tea."

Notes: 1) ferocious 兇猛的 2) unconscious 無意識的 3) succumb 屈從

10 今日有水厄 Today I Will Suffer From Flood Water

Again

In standard Chinese, the word "tea" is pronounced "cha（茶）". During the Song Dynasty, words "shui'e（水厄，flood water）" substituted "cha（茶）." Why did people in those days call tea "shui'e" or "flood water"？

At that time, there was a man named Wang Meng（王蒙）who had a passion for tea. He would invite anyone passing his house to enter and spend a bit of time drinking tea.

Afraid of hurting Wang's earnest feeling, passers would accept his invitation and drink tea with Wang. Those who were fond of tea didn't feel bad, but those who disliked tea would knit their brows while drinking.

As days went by, whenever hearing of Wang's hospitality, people would joke with each other saying, "Today I will suffer from 'flood water' again."

Notes: 1) standard 標準 2) passion 熱情 3) earnest 誠摯的；熱心的 4) knit 皺（眉） 5) brow 眉

11 貢茶可做官 You Can Secure an Official Position by Presenting a Tribute Tea

Emperor Yang Jian of the Sui Dynasty（隋文帝楊堅）once had a nightmare, in which a celestial being broke his skull, just after he ascended the throne.Following that night, he frequently suffered from headaches which the imperial medical doctors found impossible to cure.

Later, the emperor met a Buddhist monk who told him, "Some tea plants grow on the mountain. Pick the tea leaves, boil them, and drink the tea water. Your

Majesty's headaches will then disappear."

The emperor had someone go and pick tea leaves and drank the tea water based on the monk's advice. As expected, the tea really was able make the emperor's headaches and pain gradually go away. The emperor granted the monk a handsome reward for his timely advice and from that time on, the emperor kept drinking tea every day.

Accordingly, some people presented the emperor good teas in order to be granted personal favours. Those who offered tea often got promoted to higher positions in the government or became rich. At that time, there was scornful saying,

"What is the use of thoroughly studying the Spring and Autumn Annals（《春秋》）and Book of Changes（《周易》）？What would be better is to send a carriage of tea to the emperor who will offer you an official post or promote you to a higher position."

Notes: 1) nightmare 噩夢 2) skull 頭顱 3) headache 頭痛 4) thorough 徹底的

12 你命不如他 Your Fate Is Not As Good As His

In the early Ming Dynasty Emperor Zhu Yuanzhang（朱元璋）would go for a walk after dinner. One day, after his dinner, the emperor walked aimlessly into the imperial college where he sat down and his kitchen servant gave him a cup of fragrant tea.

The emperor gulped down the tea to quench his thirst after drinking wine during dinner. The tea tasted very pure to him. He asked for another cup of tea. After the second cup, the emperor became completely relaxed and happy, as if he had left the world and had become an immortal. The cups of tea brought the emperor joy, and he had his men give the servant a valuable cap and belt.

The gift presentation caused a scandal among college students. Everyone complained about the unfair treatment. A person deliberately recited a piece of poems loudly in the college yard. He said, "Study hard for ten years alone under the window; it is not worth a cup of tea still!（十載寒窗苦讀下，何如一盞茶！）"

The emperor laughed to himself and humorously responded, "You may have more ability than he has, but his luck is better!（他才不如你，你命不如他！）"

Notes: 1) aimlessly 無目的地 2) quench 解（渴） 3) relax 放鬆 4) valuable 有價值的 5) complain 抱怨6) deliberately 有意地 7) humorously 富於幽默地

13 貢茶的起源 Origin of Tribute Teas

The origin of tribute teas in Chinese history and society is closely linked to the establishment of the ancient feudal system. Like other tribute items, tribute teas served to uphold the feudal emperors' leadership over regional areas.

According to historical records, tribute tea arose during the reign of the Zhou Dynasty Wu Emperor（周武王）（770 BC—221 BC）. Emperor Wu sent his army to attack Zhou（紂）, the last king of the Yin Dynasty（16th to 11th Century BC）, where the troops from the states of the Ba and Shu（巴蜀）assisted King Wu. The two states also provided teas and other items as tribute.

In order to make local teas suitable for tribute, tea makers of all the past dynasties did their utmost to advance the technology of tea processing and in this way constantly improved the quality of tea. Although this development was driven by the need to satisfy the imperial families and the upper classes, the frequent tea exchanges between the court palace and local people enriched the country's tea culture.

Apart from the compulsory tea tribute system, some tea presenters from local areas voluntarily offered teas to emperors in order to make local products better known and more popular. These teas had local character, and the presenters hoped their local teas could gain national fame as tribute teas.

The tea tribute system lasted until the end of the Qing Dynasty.

Notes: 1) regional 地區的　2) suitable 適當的　3) do utmost 竭力�；盡全力 4) constantly 經常　5) compulsory 必須做的　6) voluntarily 志願地

14 唐代貢茶　Tang Dynasty Tribute Teas

In the Tang Dynasty, the tea tribute became more and more compulsory as tea brewing technology improved.

During the early Tang Dynasty the tribute tea was collected along with other products from local areas. Beginning in the Kaiyuan period（開元年間）, imperial families increasingly demanded larger quantities of better quality tribute tea. Some local officials made every effort to recommend their local high quality tea in order to seek promotion in office. Those factors influenced procedures for processing tribute teas.

The Tang court government set up an institution to process tribute teas at Guzhu Hill in Changxing County, Zhejiang province（長興顧渚山）. The government designated production bases for the collection of tribute teas in some counties in Hubei, Sichuan, Shaanxi, Jiangsu, Zhejiang, Fujian, Jiangxi, Hunan, Anhui, and Henan. The Supplement to the History of the Tang Dynasty（《唐國史補》）listed more than ten nationally famous teas, including "Shihua Tea from Mengding Hill（蒙頂石花）," "Zisun Tea from Guzhu Hill（顧渚紫筍）," and "Luya Tea from Fang Hill（方山露芽）," "Huangya Tea from Huo County（霍山黃芽）".

Notes: 1) recommend 推薦　2) promotion 提升　3) supplement 補充

15 宋代貢茶 Song Dynasty Tribute Teas

In the Song Dynasty, the tea tribute was further developed with respect to quality and quantity after Fujian became an important source of processed tribute teas.

In 977, the Song court government set up an official institution to process tribute teas at the foot of Fenghuang Hill（鳳凰山）in Jian'an County〔建安, modern Jian'ou County（建甌縣）, Fujian province〕. A large field of tribute tea was planted on the northern side of Fenghuang Hill. The government would send officials every year to Fenghuang Hill where they supervised the collection and processing of teas. Tea from the northern side of the hill was reserved exclusively for imperial families.

At this time tribute teas were categorized as tuan-bing tea（團餅茶）. What is tuanbing tea? It is a kind of compressed tea in the shape of a round cake. Traditionally a tuanbing tea producer usually uses wooden pestle to pound fresh tea leaves into a cake shape. Afterwards he bakes teacakes in order to preserve them. When drinking, a tuanbing tea drinker pounds a tea cake to pieces first, puts them into a kettle, and then fills the kettle with boiling hot water.In addition, the drinker may add spring onions, ginger, and oranges to improve the taste.

In the Song Dynasty each tuanbing tea cake from Jian'an County used different design to enhance their appearance. Tribute tuanbing tea cakes, made with tea leaves from the northern side of the hill, appeared with dragon and phoenix patterns on the surface, and thus named as "Dragon and Phoenix Tuanbing Tea Cakes（龍團鳳餅）." Tuanbing tea cakes produced for common people were forbidden to use the dragon and phoenix symbol.

In the Song Dynasty, the production of tribute tuan bing tea usually went through several following steps.

① Steam and wash tea leaves.

② Repeatedly squeeze the tea leaves in order to eliminate any bitter flavor.

③ Grind the squeezed tea leaves with spring water.

④ Put ground tea into a moulding presser to compress and shape. The presser's interior was engraved with dragon and phoenix patterns.

⑤ Bake the shaped tea cakes over a low fire temperature until they become completely dry.

Along with the development of tribute teas, tea presenters did their utmost to make innovative patterns and designs for the tuanbing tea in order to satisfy high-ranking officials and imperial families. Newly branded tribute tuanbing tea, patterned with the dragon and phoenix, were being constantly created.According to historical records, more than 40 kinds of tuanbing tea were designated for tribute. Most tea names sounded auspicious to the ear and were pleasing to the eye.Examples include "Longevity and Dragon Bud Leaves（萬壽龍芽），" "Dragon Tuanbing Tea Overwhelmed with Snow（龍團勝雪），" "Jade Bud Leaves in the Imperial Garden（御苑玉芽），" and "Auspicious Clouds to Circle the Dragon in Heaven（瑞雲翔龍），" to name a few.

Notes: 1) exclusive 唯一的 2) categorize 分類 3) pestle 研杵 4) preserve 保護 5) kettle 水壺 6) squeeze 擠出 7) compress 壓緊；壓縮

16 元朝貢茶 Yuan Dynasty Tribute Teas

In the Yuan Dynasty, tuanbing tea（團餅茶）was still considered tribute tea. Common people tended to drink san tea（散茶）or mo tea（末茶）. San tea literally means "loose tea," which refers to the teas'uncompressed and indistinct shape. Mo tea literally means "powder tea," which is grounded from "loose tea."

Song imperial tea production bases and tea processing institutions continued to exist during the Yuan Dynasty. In 1302 the court government established a tea plantation named "Imperial Tea Garden（御茶園）" on Wuyi Mountain（武夷山）. Wuyi Mountain became a key provider of tribute tea for the Yuan court palace.

In the Yuan Dynasty, the imperial families were the Mongols. The top administrative posts at all levels of the government were reserved for Mongols. The Mongol rulers drank tea, but they demanded less tribute tea, thereby somewhat weakening the tribute tea system.

According to historical records, there were more than 50 well-known teas from local areas, including "Shiru Tea from Wuyi Mountain（武夷山石乳），" "Dabaling Tea from Yuezhou（岳州大巴陵），" "Yuqian and Yuhou Teas from Jingzhou（荊湖雨前、雨後），" among others.

Notes: 1) uncompressed 未被壓縮的　2) indistinct 不清楚的　3) Mongol 蒙古族　4) weaken 減弱

17 寺僧與茶　Buddhist Monks and Tea

In ancient China tea bushes grew around Buddhist monasteries located on mountains and in valleys. During the Sui and Tang dynasties many Buddhist monasteries dotted China, and these monasteries organized their own sustenance where the tea industry served as a necessity. This was especially true in the south, where almost all monasteries grew tea, and tea drinking flourished among monks.

Even in the Jin Dynasty, tea already served as a common beverage among Daoist priests and Buddhist monks. Lu Yu（陸羽，733—804 AD）of the Tang Dynasty cited several cases in his work, The Book of Tea（《茶經》），which was the first book about tea in China. Each case described the tea drinking experience among Daoist priests or Buddhist monks dating back to the period between 265 and

581.

Buddhism advocates drinking tea. Buddhist doctrines explain that tea supports monastic rules in the following three ways.

① Tea helps monks stay awake to maintain meditation throughout the night.

②Tea helps digest food.

③Tea helps suppress sexual desires.

In ancient times, monks in their monasteries engaged in daily Buddhist worship rituals, as well as physical labour, which included growing and processing tea. When they were not working in the fields, some monks might try to find the best way to brew and taste tea. Monasteries were the only places that could provide such conditions for the study of tea during ancient times. Scholars composed poems or proses to illustrate their sublime tea drinking experience in monasteries. One of them was the Tang Dynasty scholar, Cao Song（曹松）. The following are some lines from his poem, Staying Overnight in Xiseng Monastery（《宿溪僧院》）:

When a young man stays in Yunxi,

His meditative mood makes him more relaxed at night;

A monk brews tea to host the quiet visitor,

Who leans against the moon and sits on the blue hill.

（少年雲溪裡，禪心夜更閒；煎茶留靜者，靠月坐蒼山。）

The tea ceremony originated in China, and Lu Yu（陸羽）is considered the founder of the Chinese tea ceremony. When he was a child, Lu Yu was adopted and brought up by a Zen master in Xidang Monastery（西　寺）. During his stay in the monastery, Lu Yu's main responsibility was to brew tea for his master, and gradually he obtained enough skill to pick tea leaves and cook them.His book systematically illustrates how to organize a tea plantation and process tea leaves, as well as

brewing and drinking tea.His writing played a major role in helping to develop the tea ceremony during its early stages. Furthermore, the initial tea ceremony gradually spread into monasteries, where many other Buddhist monks accepted his way of tea cooking and drinking.

The tea ceremony in monasteries is a ritual. Monastaries usually have a tea hall or a small teahouse, which serves as a place where monks debate Buddhist theories or host alms donors.In addition, the "tea chief"（茶頭）takes care of services related to the ritual, such as boiling water, brewing tea, and presenting tea to guests. The tea in monasteries is also used to honor Buddhist images.

There exists a saying, "Good tea grows on famous mountains; well-known monasteries produce famous tea（名山出好茶，名寺出名茶）." According to historical records and folk tales, some well-known teas originated in monasteries in ancient times.For example, "Mengding Tea"（蒙頂茶）from Mingshan Hill in Sichuan is also called "Celestial Tea（仙茶）". This tea was planted by Puhui, a Han Dynasty Zen master（普慧禪師）from Ganlu Monastery（甘露寺）. People believe that the traditional Wuyi Yan Tea（武夷岩茶）comes from Wuyi Mountain. In ancient times, local monks there would pick tea leaves in different seasons and process the leaves into three different famous teas: "Shouxing Mei Tea（longevity eyebrow tea，壽星眉），" "Lianzi Xin Tea（lotus seed tea, 蓮子心）" and "Fengwei Longxu Tea（phoenix tail and dragon beard tea，鳳尾龍鬚）."

Notes: 1) sustenance 維持；供養　2) flourish 繁茂；興旺　3) doctrine 教義 4) meditation 冥想　5) digest 消化　6) sublime 卓越的　7) systematically 有系統地

18 茶與待客　Tea and Reception

1.待客茶為先。

Tea comes first when entertaining guests.

2.茶好客常來。

Visitors will often come if the tea is good.

3.來客無煙茶，算個啥人家。

If no cigarettes or tea are offered to visitors, they will wonder what kind of family this is.

4.人走茶就涼。

Tea becomes cold after visitors depart. (This proverb reflects the inconstancy of human relationships or out of power, out of favor.)

5.酒滿敬人，茶滿傷人。

To offer a full glass of wine honors the guest; to offer a full glass of tea, however, shows disrespect.

6.君子之交淡如水，茶人之交醇如茶。

The friendship between gentlemen appears indifferent but is pure like water; the friendship between tea drinkers appears mildly intoxicated but is flavorful like tea.

7.客來敬茶。

Present a visitor with a cup of tea when he arrives.

8.好茶敬上賓，次茶等常客。

Good tea is presented to distinguished guests; common tea entertains frequent visitors.

9.客從遠方來，多以茶相待。

Tea is often presented to a visitor who comes from afar.

10.清茶一杯，親密無間。

A cup of green tea makes relationship more intimate.

11.無茶不成儀。

There is no ritual without tea.

Notes: indifferent 冷淡的

19 茶馬交易 Tea-Horse Trade

The tea-horse trade started in the Tang Dynasty, but people at that time did not regard selling horses as a stable trade.In the early Song Dynasty, people from inland regions mainly used copper coins to purchase horses from ethnic groups residing in the borderland areas. Later, herdsmen in these areas melted down copper coins and forged them into weapons. In 983, in order to maintain dynasty security and monetary dignity, the Song government issued a ban against the use of copper coins to purchase horses. Instead, cloth, silk, tea, or medicinal materials were to be used to barter for horses.

In order to help the border trade continue smoothly, the Song government also set up a tea-horse department（茶馬司）to take care of the profits gained from tea business monopoly and supervise the tea-horse trade.

Accordingly, Song horse markets were estab-lished in several places on the present day areas of Shanxi, Gansu, and Sichuan.Horse markets from Sichuan were involved in the tea-horse trade with southwest ethnic nationalities. The purchased horses were mainly used for hard labour. The markets in Shanxi, Shaanxi, and Gansu purchased horses from northwest ethnic nationalities mainly for battle steeds.

In the Yuan Dynasty there was no shortage of horses in China. Tea was exchanged during this period with silver or local products. In the early Ming

Dynasty the tea-horse trade markets resumed and continued until the middle period of the Qing Dynasty. These markets were then gradually closed down.

Notes: 1) borderland 邊境 2) herdsman 牧民 3) steed 駿馬 4) resume 恢復

20 茶文化向邊疆各族的傳播 Tea Spreads to the Ethnic Nationality Borderland Areas

During Chinese tea history, tea spread from inland regions to borderland areas where ethnic groups resided.

Tibetans eat lots of meat every day, so tea helps them to digest the meat. Thus according to historical records, tea came to the Tibetan region in the Tang Dynasty. In 641 Princess Wencheng（文成公主）went to Tibet where she married the Tubo King, Songtsan Gampo（吐蕃松贊干布）. Tea was one of her dowry items.

During mid-Tang Dynasty, when imperial court envoys visited the Tibetan Kings, they often saw in local Tibetan chieftains' houses some well known kinds of tea grown and processed in ancient inland China. Following the mid-Tang Dynasty, the tea-horse trade further promoted the relationships between the Tibetan regime and Central Plains.

During the Tang Dynasty a nomadic ethnic nationality called Huihe（回紇）lived in ancient Northwest China. More than a thousand Huihe businessmen resided in Chang'an（長安）, the Tang Dynasty capital, where they studied or did business.

According to historical records, Huihe businessmen would drive horses to markets to barter for tea. After purchasing tea, they kept some for their own consumption and then traded the rest with Turks and Arabs for profit.

The Western Xia Regime（西夏，1038—1227）appeared in ancient Northwest China during the early Song Dynasty. This regime was mainly composed

of the Dangxiang people（党項族）that grew out of a branch of the Qiang ethnic nationality.They raised horses, sheep, and camels and also engaged in trade. During the early Song Dynasty the Dangxiang people sold their horses to the Song businessmen who purchased them with copper coins. The Dangxiang people used these coins to cast weapons. In 983 the Song government issued a ban against the use of copper coins to purchase horses.Instead of coins, people started to barter for horses with tea and other products.

During the early years of the Western Xia state, the Song imperial court often presented its rulers with gifts of silver, silk, cloth, tea, and the like. The volume of tea reached thousands of jin（斤）. In 1038 Yuan Hao（元昊）proclaimed himself the Western Xia Emperor. He launched wars against the Song Dynasty, leading to great losses on both sides. The Western Xia Regime and the Song court later agreed to cease fighting and afterwards peacefully coexisted. Although Yuan Hao submitted to the Song, the Song court was forced to pay a costly annual tribute of silver, silk, and tea. The volume of tea went up to several tens of thousands of jin, and at times even exceeded that amount.

The Nüzhens, or Jurchens（女真族）, were an ancient ethnic nationality that was based farther north in ancient northeastern China and swallowed up the Liao Regime（遼國，907—1125）. In 1126 they overwhelmed the Song capital at Kaifeng. With their own capital near Beijing, they set up a dynasty known as the Jin（金）, meaning "gold." A treaty was drawn up with the Southern Song, and the Jin Dynasty asserted seniority over the Southern Song, demanding the payment of tribute, which was handed over in the form of silk, tea, and silver.

Gradually, the Jin people learned the art of tea-drinking from the Song. Day after day, tea-drinking became more popular among the Jin people, including court members, scholars, and common people. Many teahouses appeared in towns and cities, and scholars considered tea equal to wine.

When tea consumption got out of control, the Jin court issued a ban several times against tea-drinking. The court feared that such consumption might weaken the dynasty's economy and military defence. Although the ban was very strict, tea-drinking continued in non-governmental communities.

Notes: 1) dowry 嫁妝 2) envoy 特使 3) nomadic 遊牧的 4) consumption 消耗 5) be composed of 由⋯⋯組成 6) coexist 共存 7) exceed 超過 8) assert 聲稱

21 廣州人的早茶文化 Morning Tea Culture in Guangzhou

Morning tea in Guangzhou involves going to teahouses to drink tea and have a light breakfast. With their pleasant interior dcors, local teahouses serve as places for a social occasion, providing tea and variety of snacks. Customers get together by twos and threes, drinking tea and eating food while chatting. This custom is a traditional method for enhancing the pleasure of tea drinking, reinforcing friendships and establishing new personal, political, or business relations.

Traditionally no exquisite procedure is required when local people in Guangzhou drink tea in teahouses. Only guests will lightly tap the tabletop with their fore and middle fingers when the host pours tea for them. The finger tapping expresses their appreciation to the host.

Tea drinking service in Guangzhou's teahouses is usually classified as "early morning tea," "afternoon tea" and "evening tea." The morning tea usually starts at 4 o'clock in the early morning; and the evening tea runs until 1 or 2 o'clock in the morning of the next day. Some teahouses are open all night.

The morning tea generally runs from the early morning until 11 o'clock. The teahouses are often full of customers during that period. On weekends or in holidays, customers may have to wait in line outside teahouses. "The evening tea" also tends to be popular. This is especially the case during the summer, when teahouses are the first daily attraction for local people.

When people in Guangzhou are free, they enjoy brewing "gongfu tea（功夫茶）" at home. Gongfu literally means "learnt skilled" and is a philosophy applied to any time-honoured pursuit of excellence.The gongfu teapot appears as small as a fist in size, and a tiny cup only as large as a table-tennis ball in half size. Local people prefer Oolong Tea when they brew "gongfu tea." Usually the server first puts Oolong Tea leaves in a teapot and then fills the teapot with hot boiled water. The server drains the water immediately, leaving the leaves behind. The draining is repeated one or two times for the practical purpose of washing the leaves. Then the server pours the tea to the tiny cups one after another continuously. Each cup of tea is expected to have the same flavor. After the procedure is completed, people start to savor the tea while exchanging local gossip.

Notes: 1) interior d cor 室內裝修 2) reinforce 加強 3) exquisite 精緻的 4) attraction 吸引力 5) server 侍者；上菜者 6) drain 排出（液體） 7) savor 品味 8) gossip 閒談

22 中國飲茶方法的四次較大改變 The Four Major Developments in Chinese Tea Drinking Methods

China has a tea culture that goes back thousands of years. Through the centuries, Chinese people have continually improved their tea-drinking methods as tea-processing technology advanced. The following four major developments have occurred in the history of Chinese tea drinking.

The Initial Change: Tea Leaves Decoction

In primitive clan society our ancestors did not have enough food to eat because of low agricultural productivity. They picked and ate wild tea leaves as food because the leaves were edible and had no poison. They ate these leaves only to satisfy their hunger.

People discovered that tea leaves offered greater benefits, including quenching thirst, driving away summer heat, and even counteracting poison. Gradually tea was taken as a medicine rather eaten to supplement the diet. At this stage, people usually boiled the tea leaves to extract juice to cure diseases. Boiling the tea leaves to extract the flavor can be seen as the first step in tea drinking. Tea served as a medicine or as a sacrificial item offered at the altars erected for the dead or deities.

The Second Development: Tea Porridge

From the primitive times to the Han Dynasty, tea gradually evolved into a daily beverage. At that time, when people boiled tea, they usually added millet rice and flavoured seasonings, and continued boiling it until the tea water had been turned into a thin porridge. This method still remained popular during the Tang Dynasty. And some ethnic nationalities in the outlying areas of China currently still keep this tradition alive by adding some food to tea water.

The Third Development: Tuanbing Tea Drinking

The third tea drinking method appeared in the Three Kingdoms Period and prevailed in the Tang Dynasty and flourished in the Song Dynasty. Tea producers would pick tea leaves and pound them into a cake shape. When drinking, they would pound a teacake to pieces, put them into a kettle, and then fill the kettle with boiling hot water. At that time, they added ginger, oranges, and other seasonings.

In the middle period of the Tang Dynasty, Lu Yu（陸羽）, author of The Book of Tea（《茶經》）, firmly opposed to adding any seasonings, and instead emphasized that everyone should taste pure tea with no other additives. Tang Dynasty Chinese people called this way of drinking pure tea "qingming（清茗）." "Qing" means "pure；" "ming" "tender tea leaves." After

drinking "pure tea," drinkers would chew the boiled leaves to further appreciate its flavour.

During the Song Dynasty people gradually brewed " pure tea. " Eating tea porridge gradually disappeared save for some outlying areas.

The Fourth Development: Whole Piece Tea Drinking

Drinking whole pieces of tea leaves started in the Tang Dynasty and flourished in the Ming and Qing dynasties. In the Tang Dynasty, people found a way to make loose tea（散茶）through steaming and baking processing; they tended to brew whole piece tea leaves with hot boiled water. In the Song Dynasty the practice of drinking whole piece tea leaves coexisted with tuanbing tea drinking. In the Ming Dynasty tea producers primarily made "loose tea," and people usually brewed tea with whole piece tea leaves. This whole piece tea leaves drinking method has continued up through now. Most modern people drink tea this way.

Notes: 1) initial 最初的 2) productivity 生產力 3) extract 提取 4) outlying 邊遠的 5) additive 附加的；添加物 6) chew 嚼 7) tend to 傾向於 8) primarily 主要地

23 茶與婚禮 Tea and Marriage

Tea serves as an essential part of wedding ceremonies.In 641 Princess Wencheng（文成公主）went to Tibet where she married Tubo King Songtsan Gambo（吐蕃松贊干布）. She brought tea to Tibet as one of her dowries.

In the Tang Dynasty tea drinking prevailed and also served as an indispensable marriage gift. In the Song Dynasty the tea dowry turned to be a betrothal gift presented to the family of the bride-to-be at the engagement.In most cases during the Yuan and Ming dynasties, the word "chali (tea gift, 茶禮)" sounded synonymous with "marriage." The word "chicha (drink tea, 喫茶)" refers to "tea gift" being accepted by a prospective daughter-in-law from an unmarried boy's family. The tea gift acceptance by the girl's family was the prevailing custom of marriage of that time. This custom still survived during the Qing Dynasty.

These traditional terms are still currently in use in some rural areas of China. In such places terms like "shoucha（tea gift acceptance，受茶）" refer to "marriage engagement," "chajin（tea money，茶金）" to "down payment at the engagement," and chali（茶禮）to "betrothal gift."

During the traditional wedding ceremony, tea is an essential part of entertaining guests. The bride and groom usually kneel before their parents and serve them tea to express their gratitude.

Notes: 1) essential 必要的 2) betrothal 訂婚 3) gratitude 感激

酒典故與趣談 Interesting Stories About Chinese Alcoholic Beverages

1 酒池肉林 Alcohol Pool and Meat Forest

Almost all the kings of late Shang Dynasty invariably pursued the enjoyment of pleasure and comfort. The same could be said of the Shang aristocrats, who would drink to excess on many occasions. According to The Records of the Grand Historian（《史記》）by Sima Qian（司馬遷）, Zhou, the last king of the Shang Dynasty, had a strong affection for women and alcoholic drinks. "King Zhou had his men use a pool to contain alcoholic beverages and hang pieces of meat extensively like a forest, and in the forest and pool he made naked men and women chase after one another to accompany his all night drinking（〈紂〉以酒為池，縣〈懸〉肉為林，使男女裸相逐其間，為長夜之飲。）." In the following generations, "alcohol pool and meat forest" implies "a luxurious life and constant indulgence in carnal pleasure without restraint."

Many cases of over indulgence in alcohol that occurred in ancient times resulted in the disruption of an opportunity for combat in battle fields. The army led by King Gong of the State of Chu（楚恭王）once fought a battle at Yanling（鄢陵）against the army from the State of Jin（晉國）. The Chu army was defeated and an arrow hit King Gong on the eye. As King Gong was preparing for his counterattack, he summoned General Zifan（子反）to discuss strategy and tactics. However, he was told that Zifan was drunk and could not meet with him. The king

sighed in despair, saying "My army is doomed to failure（天敗我也）." The Chu army and the king had to withdraw from the battlefield. Zifan was executed because his drinking caused him to neglect his military duty.

Notes: 1) invariably 不變地 2) pursue 追隨 3) aristocrat 貴族 4) excess 過度 5) affection 影響 6) alcoholic 酒精的 7) beverage 飲料 8) naked 裸體的 9) indulgence 沉溺 10) carnal 淫蕩的 11) restraint 抑制 12) disruption 崩潰 13) counterattack 反攻 14) summon 傳喚 15) withdraw 收回；撤退

2 鴻門宴 Hongmen Banquet

Toward the end of the Qin Dynasty Liu Bang（劉邦）and Xiang Yu（項羽）led their troops to fight against the Qin army. Liu's troops occupied Xianyang（咸陽）, capital of the Qin Dynasty, ahead of Xiang's army. Upon hearing of this news, Xiang Yu was furious. He moved his troops forward and stationed them in Hongmen, close to Xinfeng Town（新豐鴻門）in the Xianyang area; Liu Bang stationed his troops at Bashang（霸上）. At that time, Xiang's troops appeared much stronger than Liu's.

One of Liu Bang's assistants, Cao Wushang（曹無傷）, delivered a message to Xiang Yu, saying that Liu Bang intended to proclaim himself king of Guanzhong（關中）, which was located in present-day Shaanxi. Upon hearing this, Xiang Yu became even angrier. He ordered all his soldiers to have breakfast early the next morning and then march against Liu's army.

A great battle ensued. Liu immediately persuaded Xiang Bo（項伯）, Xiang Yu's uncle, to mediate between the two sides. Xiang Bo agreed and also invited Liu Bang to go to Hongmen to meet Xiang Yu the next day.

The following morning, Xiang Yu held a banquet to entertain Liu Bang. Although good alcoholic beverages and various delicacies were provided, the atmosphere was tense because Fan Zeng（范增）, Xiang Yu's adviser, repeatedly gave signs to Xiang Yu to kill Liu Bang in the banquet. Xiang Yu hesitated. Fan Zeng then arranged for Xiang Zhuang（項莊）to perform a sword-dance in front of the participants under the pretence of livening up their drinking and eating. Actually, Xiang Zhuang intended to kill Liu Bang when the opportunity presented itself. While the ceremony was going on, Xiang Bo pulled out his sword to play the same sword-dance together with Xiang Zhuang and protect Liu Bang with his own body.

At a critical moment, Fan Kuai（樊噲）, Liu Bang's subordinate, took his sword and burst into the banquet room where he fiercely stared at Xiang Yu. When Xiang Yu discovered Fan Kuai was a warrior responsible for Liu Bang's security service, Xiang Yu immediately presented a glass of wine to Fan Kuai. Fan Kuai stood and drank the glass. Xiang Yu then presented him with a pork leg, asking him if he could drink more. Fan Kuai said, "How could a humble subject refuse a glass of wine since he is willing even to die（臣死且不避, 卮酒安足辭？）"

Fan Kuai seized the opportunity to list a number of Liu Bang's merits and contributions to the downfall of the Qin Dynasty. Xiang Yu had nothing to say in reply. Liu Bang took advantage of this opportunity to walk away and return to his troops.

Later, people refer to the Hongmen Banquet as a feast or meeting set up as a trap for those invited.

Notes: 1) assistant 助手 2) persuade 説服 3) atmosphere 氣氛 4) hesitate 猶豫不決 5) under the pretence of 以……為藉口 6) liven up 使有生氣 7) subordinate 下屬 8) fiercely 兇猛地

3 魯酒薄而邯鄲圍 Handan Is Besieged due to Ordinary Wine from the State of Lu

This story occurred when King Xuan of the State of Chu（楚宣王，369 BC—340 BC）met with representatives from various kingdoms. Duke Gong, from the State of Lu（魯國恭公）, was late for the meeting. Moreover, his gift of alcoholic beverages tasted just ordinary, which made King Xuan extremely unhappy.

Duke Gong said, "I am a descendant of the Zhou imperial family, and my personal status is of royal nobility. Now I have disgraced my dignity by presenting you with alcoholic beverages. To make matters worse, you blamed me for my beverages, saying that it tasted average. You have gone too far."

As a result, King Xuan Wang sought an alliance with the State of Qi, in an attempt to start a war against the State of Lu. At the time the king of Qi was considering an attack against the State of Zhao（趙國）. However, he hesitated because he feared that Chu might back up Zhao. It was at this time that Chu asked Qi for help, which relieved the king of Qi of his fear. Therefore, the State of Qi joined in the alliance with Chu. At the same time, the troops from Qi attacked the State of Zhao and occupied its capital, Handan. The Zhao unfortunately became the victim because of the ordinary alcoholic beverages offered by Duke Gong from the State of Lu.

Notes: 1) representative 代表　2) descendant 後裔　3) nobility 貴族　4) disgrace 恥辱　5) alliance 聯盟　6) unfortunately 令人遺憾地

4 箪醪勞師　Reward an Army with Alcohol in a Bamboo Utensil

In the Spring and Autumn Period（春秋時代）, the army from the State of Wu（吳國）destroyed the State of Yue（越國）. In order to take revenge and restore the State of Yue, Gou Jian（勾踐）, the Yue State's King, issued an order encouraging people to bear more children. He even used wine as a prize to honor those who gave birth to children. The order said, "Two pots of alcohol and one dog are rewarded to those who give birth to a boy; two pots of alcohol and one pig to those who give birth to a girl（生丈夫，二壺酒，一犬；生女子，二壺酒，一豚）."

After King Gou Jian completed preparation for revenge, he decided to attack the State of Wu. Just before he departed with his army, the Yue State's elders offered good wine to King Gou Jian. The king poured out all the wine into the upper reaches of a river, so that he could share the wine with his soldiers by drinking the river water mixed with wine together with them. His conduct greatly enhanced the morale of his soldiers.

Notes: 1) take revenge 報仇　2) reward 報酬　3) pour out 倒；灌　4) enhance 提高　5) morale 士氣

5 漢高祖醉斬白蛇 Liu Bang Slaughtered a White Snake while Drunk

According to The Records of the Grand Historian written by Sima Qian, Liu Bang served as a community head during the late years of Qin Dynasty. Once he took charge of sending labourers away to Mountain Li（驪山）, but many of the labourers died on their journey. When they reached the west part of Fengyi County that was close to a pool（豐西澤）, Liu Bang released all the labourers after a drinking binge. As a result, only about ten labourers remained to accompany him.

That same night, Liu Bang and his men continued their journey, crossing over the pool even though he was drunk. Liu Bang asked one man to go ahead to scout the way.

Soon the man returned, saying that a big snake stood in their way and forced them to make a hasty retreat. Liu Bang's intoxication had made him fearless, so he

said, "Follow me! This is nothing to be afraid of!" They bravely advanced, and Liu Bang cut the snake into two parts with his sword. Then they continued their trip for miles until Liu Bang fell into a drunken stupor.

Shortly after this happened, an old woman wept on the scene where the snake had been slaughtered. Someone asked her why she wept there. The old woman said, "Someone slaughtered my son."

"How did you know that your son was slaughtered?" another man asked.

"My child was the son of the White King, and he turned into the snake. He was slaughtered by the son of the Red King because my child blocked his way."

Later, someone told Liu Bang what the woman said. Upon hearing the story, Liu Bang felt proud of his deed.

Notes: 1) community 社區 2) take charge of 負責 3) labourer 體力勞動者 4) release 釋放

6 清聖濁賢 Light Sage and Strong Person of Virtue

During the early years of the Wei Kingdom of the Three Kingdoms Period, its Emperor, Cao Cao（曹操）, prohibited the drinking of alcohol. People in the kingdom had to secretly drink alcoholic beverages. As a result, they carefully avoided breathing the word jiu（酒，wine）. Instead, they used xianren（賢人，person of virtue）to replace the words zhuojiu（濁酒，strong wine）; shengren（聖人，sage）came to mean qingjiu（清酒，light wine）. Gradually "the light sage and strong person of virtue" developed into an indirect reference to suggest different kinds of alcoholic beverages.

There is another story that tells of the use of indirect references to evaluate the quality of alcoholic beverages. During the Eastern Jin Dynasty there was an assistant under General Huanwen（桓溫）. He was good at judging alcoholic beverages. Whenever the general got a new alcoholic drink, the assistant would be required to taste it first. If it tasted good, the assistant would say, "qingzhou congshi（an official position in Qingzhou，青州從事）." If it tasted average, he would say, "pingyuan duyou（postal superintendent in Pingyuan，平原督郵）."

Qingzhou（青州）is an area in which there is a prefecture called Qijun（齊郡）. Qi（齊）sounds the same to Qi（臍）, which means navel. Under Pingyuan（平原）there was a county called Gexian（鬲縣）. Ge（鬲）sounds the same to Ge（膈）, which is "the partition separating the chest and abdominal cavities." According to the assistant's explanation, good-quality drink flows all the way down to the navel, while average drink only reaches the partition separating the chest and abdominal cavities.

Notes: 1) secretly 秘密地 2) breathe 呼吸；低聲説出 3) reference 指示 4) indirect 間接的 5) evaluate 評價 6) superintendent 主管人 7) partition 劃分 8) abdominal 腹部的 9) cavity（身體的）腔

7 杯酒釋兵權 Glasses of Alcohol Lead to Change of Military Leadership

Within half a year after the founding of the Song Dynasty, Zhao Kuangyin（趙匡胤）, the first Song Emperor, had to go on an expedition in person to suppress a mutiny launched by military commanders. Although the mutiny was unsuccessful, the emperor was becoming increasingly worried that a similar mutiny that might occur in future.

One day Zhao Pu（趙普）, prime minister of the dynasty, said to him, "The basic cause of the mutiny is that the generals are in charge of military leadership. If the centralized court government holds the military leadership, people in the country will live in peace."

Before long, the emperor held a dinner party, and drank alcohol with several military generals. Being half drunk, the emperor said to them, "Without your support, I wouldn't have become the emperor. However, as I am the emperor, I feel even more uncomfortable than before. Why? Many other people also want to be emperor. I trust your loyalty, but how are you going to handle the situation if your subordinates are greedy for wealth and social position? Stimulated by this desire, they might persuade you to take the throne even if you are unwilling to do so."

After hearing these remarks, the generals began weeping. Meanwhile they said, "We are all rough fellows, so such a thought would never come into our heads. We are expecting your majesty to show us a way out."

"Well," said the emperor, "I will offer you advice. You might as well hand over the military leadership, and then I'll appoint you as high-ranking officials to work in local areas. These official positions have no actual power, but you will be able to lead a leisurely and quiet life, purchasing land and property for your children and grandchildren. At the same time, we will become relatives by marriage between our children. Does my advice sound good?"

The generals said with one voice, "Your majesty is very considerate of his humble subjects."

After the dinner party, everyone went home. The next morning these generals went to court where they each presented their written memorials to the emperor, requesting to resign from their military leadership because of sickness and old age. The emperor accepted their resignation, awarded them a large sum of property and then appointed them as high-ranking officials in different local areas.

Notes: 1) suppress 鎮壓　2) mutiny 兵變　3) centralized 中央集權的　4) leisurely 從容的　5) be considerate of 體諒　9) memorial 請願書

8 中國古代的十大宮廷貢酒　Ten Tribute Alcoholic

Beverages in Ancient China

古井貢酒 Gujing Tribute Liquor

In 196 Cao Cao presented a kind of liquor brewed in his hometown to the Han Dynasty Liu Xie Emperor（漢獻帝劉協）. Back then it was called "Jiu Yun Chun Jiu"（jiuyun rich and good alcoholic beverage，九醞春酒）. Jiuyun Chunjiu continued to be a tribute liquor during the ensuing dynasties. Its present name is Gujing Tribute Liquor. It was nominated as the famous liquor in Anhui Province in 1960, and it won the title of the Eight Top Brands in China in 1963.

鶴年貢酒 Henian Tribute Liquor

Beijing Heniantang（北京鶴年堂）was established in 1405 and played a special role in preparing medicinal wine and tea for the Ming and Qing dynasties' imperial palaces. Invited by the imperial house of alcoholic beverages, Ding Henian（丁鶴年）produced a series of Henian Tribute Liquors based on a secret recipe handed down from his family's ancestors and the principles of Chinese medicine. In 1927 a new series of Henian Tribute Liquors appeared, which were derived from the same recipe, including Jinfo Jiu（金佛酒）, Jinju Jiu（金橘酒）and others that greatly appealed to distinguished figures and scholars then living in Beijing.

棗集美酒 Zaoji Liquor

Zaoji Town（棗集鎮）in Henan is well-known across the country for its long involvement in liquor-making, which can be traced back to the Spring and Autumn Period（春秋時期）and continued to develop during the Sui and Tang dynasties.It is said that Song Zhenzong（宋真宗）, a Song Dynasty emperor, issued an imperial order nominating the local wine in Zaoji Town as a tribute liquor. The emperor's nomination illustrates the popular saying: "Heaven bestows well-known liquor, and Earth offers famous springs（天賜名酒, 地賜名泉）."

酃酒 Ling Liquor

Ling Liquor（酃酒）became a tribute liquor as early as the Northern Wei Dynasty（北魏）. Moreover, Ling Liquor was one of the best known alcoholic beverages used for sacrificial purposes when emperors of the ensuing dynasties held a memorial ceremony for their ancestors or in honor of deities.

Originally this wine was a home-made beverage produced by peasants living near Ling Lake（酃湖）, located east of present-day Hengyang City（衡陽市）, Hunan Province. Almost all of the households in the Hengyang rural area are now able to make this wine using old methods. Whenever traditional festivals occur, local people usually offer guests Ling Liquor.

鴻茅酒 Hongmao Liquor

Hongmao Liquor（鴻茅酒）first appeared in 1693 in Hongmao Town（鴻茅鎮）, Liangcheng County（涼城縣）, Inner Mongolia.In the fourth year of the Qing Dynasty Qianlong Emperor's reign（清乾隆四年）a Chinese doctor whose name was Wang Jitian（王吉天）arrived at Hongmao Town. He found the locally-made liquor to be so good in quality that he actually purchased the Hongmao Distillery. He planned to prepare Hongmao Yao Liquor（鴻茅藥酒，Hongmao Medicinal Liquor）using the local liquor from the distillery, as well as the secret recipe of herbal medicine handed down from his family's ancestors. Afterwards the local liquor was all reserved for the use of Hongmao Yao Liquor. During the Qing Dynasty Daoguang Emperor's reign（道光年間）both Hongmao Liquor and the medicinal liquor were put on the list of tribute wines.

羊羔美酒 Yanggao Wine

Yanggao means "lamb." The recipe of the wine is unique.Its ingredients include high-quality millet, tender mutton, fresh fruit, and valuable Chinese medicinal herbs. The wine has an amber color and its alcohol content is 17 %. The wine is good at offsetting yin deficiency, affects the lungs by making them less dry, and increases the body's strength or vitality. During the Tang Dynasty this wine served as a court palace tribute liquor.

汾酒 Fen Liquor

According to historical records, this liquor was on the list of tribute liquors during the Northern and Southern Dynasties. The liquor's high-quality is largely due to the pristine water from the wells located at xinghua cun（the Apricot Blossom Village，杏花村）in Shanxi Province. The following line from a Tang Dynasty poem greatly helped the village and the liquor retain its fame throughout the history of feudal China："May I ask where the liquor shop is? A shepherd boy points to the Apricot Blossom Village at a distance（借問酒家何處有，牧童遙指杏花村)."

The liquor won a gold medal at the 1916 Panama International Exhibition.

五加皮酒 Wu Jia Pi Liquor

This liquor, which is also called wu jia pi yao jiu（Wu Jia Pi Medicinal Liquor，五加皮藥酒）, is produced in Meicheng Town, Jiande County, Zhejiang Province（建德縣梅城鎮浙江省）. It is said that it first appeared during the Tang Dynasty and is one of ancient China's oldest tribute liquors. More than 20 unique Chinese medicinal herbs are added to the modern version of this liquor during the wine-making process.

菊花酒 Chrysanthemum Liquor

The chrysanthemum has traditionally symbolized vitality or "longevity." Chrysanthemum Liquor became a common Chinese liquor as early as the Han Dynasty, as well as during the Three Kingdoms Period. In ancient times people drank chrysanthemum liquor during the Double Ninth Festival because they considered it an auspicious liquor that could bring people good luck and help them avoid calamities.

The Double Ninth Festival occurs in the middle of autumn. People on that day

normally enjoy seeing the blossoming chrysanthemum flowers while drinking chrysanthemum liquor.

「同盛金」燒酒 Tongshengjin Liquor

On June 9, 1996 people accidentally found four ancient wooden liquor containers 80 centimetres underneath the Lingchuan Main Distillery's old compound in Jinzhou City, Liaoning Province（錦州凌川釀酒總廠）. The containers preserved some liquor that was still in good condition. The liquor was sealed up with xuan paper dipped in deer blood. It appeared slightly yellow in colour, and its alcohol content was 53 %. According to the evaluation by archaeological experts, the liquor was originally made and preserved by liquor-makers from the Tongshengjin Liquor Workshop（同盛金酒坊）. It dated back to the 25th year of the Qing Dynasty Daoguang Emperor's reign（清道光二十五年）.

Notes: 1) tribute 貢物 2) ensuing 接踵而至的 3) nominate 提名 4) ancestor 祖先 5) trace back to 追溯到 6) deity 神 7) rural 鄉村的 8) occur 發生 9) distillery 釀酒廠 10) millet 小米；穀子 11) amber 琥珀色的 2) deficiency 缺乏 13) vitality 活力 14) pristine 純潔的；清新的 15) exhibition 展覽會 16) process 加工 17) calamity 災害 18) centimetre 釐米 19) compound 院子 20) container 容器

9 傳統飲酒禮節 Some Alcohol Drinking Customs

女兒酒 Liquor for Daughters

N er liquor（女兒酒）means "liquor for daughters." It is said that a long time ago people in ancient South China customarily began making liquor when their daughters were born.After they completed their liquor making, they buried it beneath the bottom of a pond rather than drinking it right away. The liquor was kept there until the day of their daughter's wedding ceremony, when the daughter's parents took out the liquor to entertain guests.

It is said that this kind of wine developed into one of Shaoxing's current local liquors and is called Huadiao Liquor（花雕酒）. The container for Huadiao liquor is unique, with varied carved flowers, figures, birds, beasts, and pavilions on mountains or by rivers. During a daughter's wedding ceremony, her parents take out the liquor container, and a painter paints the carved patterns and writes some lucky words like "blooming flowers and full moon（花好月圓）" on the container to convey the parents' sincere wishes for their daughter's happiness.

喜酒 Alcoholic Beverages Drinking at a Wedding

Xijiu（喜酒）refers to "alcoholic beverages drunk during weddings." It is usually synonymous with "wedding ceremony." If someone will be participating in a wedding ceremony, he/she often says, "I am going to drink xijiu at a wedding ceremony."

會親酒 Huiqin Toast

The Huiqin toast means "sealing the marriage engagement with a toast." A dinner or even a banquet is necessary in order to complete a Chinese marriage engagement. The groom and bride's families eat together on this important day. While eating, they toast with alcoholic beverages, indicating that the marriage engage-ment has been sealed. After toasts, the marriage agreement is in force, and neither side can break off the engagement without serious repercussions.

回門酒 Huimen Toast

The second day after the wedding, a newly-married couple is scheduled to return to the home of the married woman's parents. This visit is called huimen, or return visit.On the same day, the married woman's parents usually host the visiting couple with an excellent lunch and liquor that is called huimeng jiu, the alcoholic beverage drunk for their return visit.

交杯酒 Jiaobei Toast

Jiaobei toast refers to "a toast with interlocked arms." This is a traditional courtesy to express sincere love between a husband and wife during their wedding ceremony. The jiaobei toast first appeared during the Tang Dynasty. During the Song Dynasty people often used a colourful silk ribbon to link up two cups. The newly married husband and wife each held the linked-up cups or interlocked their arms for a toast. This custom continues even till today.

滿月酒／百日酒 Manyue Toast or Bairi Toast

Manyue means "the first month of a newborn baby;" bairi "the first hundred days of the baby." In China, anywhere between a month and a hundred days after the birth of a baby, the baby's parents usually hold a feast to entertain relatives and friends who come on this occasion. Visitors present gifts and exchange liquor toasts with wishes for the baby's good fortune.

壽酒 Longevity Toast

People in China keep up the family tradition of expressing the best wishes to a senior member when his/her birthday occurs. The key longevity celebration takes place when a senior reaches the age of 50, 60 or 70 years old. Usually his/her children or grandchildren hold a feast. Relatives and friends are aslo invited to this banquet. They make toasts for the senior's happy birthday.

上樑酒／進屋酒

Roof-Beam-Placement Toast or New-House Dwel-ling Toast

In Chinese rural areas, building a new house is a major undertaking for a peasant. One of main proce-dures when constructing a house is placing beams on the roof of the dwelling. Accordingly, the new homeowner usually provides good food and liquor to entertain all the workmen on the roof-beam placement day. The host exchanges toasts with the workers for the successful beam placement. In some rural areas, a craftsman sprays the beams with alcoholic drinks.

After the house is built the family moves into the new dwelling, the host holds another feast to celebrate the new house's completion. At the same time, the host and his family offer a sacrificial ceremony to please the deities or obtain their ancestors' blessing.

Notes: 1) indicate 表明　2) a newly-married couple 新婚夫妻　3) interlock 使連接　4) courtesy 禮貌　5) ribbon 緞帶　6) undertaking 任務；事業　7) procedure 程序　8) construction 建設　9) craftsman 工匠

10 獨特的飲酒方式 Unique Ways of Drinking Alcohol

轉轉酒　Zhuanzhuan Drinking

Zhuan means "turn around." Zhuanzhuan drinking is a unique way of alcoholic drinking among people of the Yi ethnic nationality in Southwest China. No matter whether they are guests or hosts, people habitually sit in a circle around a jar that contains an alcoholic beverage. They drink together with only a cup or glass, which passes around from one participant's hand to another one's. Each drinks a very small quantity or just sips his drink at a time when he holds the cup in order to stay sober and properly behave himself in the circle.

勸酒　Persuade Others to Drink More

Chinese hosts always want their guests to drink more. On special occasions, like a dinner banquet or feast, they repeatedly invite their guests for toasts in a hospitable attempt to overwhelm the guests with alcoholic beverages. The more the guests drink, the happier is the host.It is not a guest's job to drink himself or herself to the point of discomfort, but if the guest drinks too little, this may also upset the host.

文敬　A Toast in a Gentle Way

As the beginning of a dinner party, a host makes the first toast after giving a short opening speech. Sometimes he will turn his glass upside down to show no liquor is left in the glass. While this happens, the guests stand up and usually drink their liquor off. During the party, the host often leaves his seat and goes to each table to clink the glasses to each guest and then drink a toast to them.

回敬 Drink a Toast in Return

As a host toasts, guests will respond. Even if the host or some other participants propose a "sip" toast, everyone in the party should do a "bottom up." Generally guests should graciously accept these gestures. Towards the end of the meal, the senior guest should give a return speech of gratitude for the hospitality and propose an appropriate toast.

互敬 Toasts Among Guests

These toasts may involve guests at the table. Usually the one who proposes the toast will give various excuses or reasons, which sound so convincing that it is hard to reject a "bottom up." Throughout toast exchanges, participants at a table continue talking with each other.

代飲 A Substitute Toast Drinker

Toasts are used not only to express interest or pleasure in the event, but also sometimes to demonstrate drinking prowess. So when a host or a guest is the "object" of numerous toasts, it is acceptable to have a substitute to drink on his behalf, since sometimes joining the toast with water or a soft drink is not desirable. For example, at the wedding party, the bridesmaid and the best man usually serve as ideal substitutes to drink wine on behalf of the bride and bridegroom.

Notes: 1) habitually 習慣性地　2) sober 清醒　3) repeatedly 反覆地　4) upset 使難過　5) graciously 有禮貌地　6) gesture 手勢；表示　7) appropriate 適當的　8) reject 拒絕　9) prowess 非凡的能力　10) acceptable 可接受的　11) substitute 代替

12) bridesmaid 伴娘　13) bridegroom 新郎

11 酒與原始宗教、祭祀、喪葬 Alcohol in Primitive Religion, Sacrificial Offering and Funeral Services

Magic is an important component of primitive religion. In ancient China sorcerers often employed alcoholic beverages in a variety of ritual ceremonies, offering sacrifices to supernatural beings both to pray for blessings and to ward off natural and man-made calamities.

Alcoholic beverages would be presented on sacrificial occasions with great respect to Heaven, the Gods, and ancestors. According to The Rites of the Zhou Dynasty（《周禮》）, there were eight kinds of beverages in use for sacrificial services. Later, an official position was created to oversee the pouring out of alcoholic beverages to honor supernatural beings during sacrificial ceremonies.

In some traditional major festivals a family usually holds a feast at home. Based on the Chinese-style seating arrangement, the seat of honour often remains unoccupied as the symbol of the place for the family's deceased ancestors. The family host, other members, and guests are accordingly seated to the left and right of the unoccupied seat in descending order of importance. As they begin placing dishes and drinks on the table, these food and alcoholic beverages usually go first to the place in front of the unoccupied seat as a conventional token of letting the ancestors eat and drink first.In front of the ancestors' images are burning candles, some dishes and drinks, which express the family's sincere memories and tribute to their ancestors.

When a person passes away, his/her relatives and friends all gather to mourn his/her death. According to Han Chinese custom, a vegetarian feast is held during the funeral ceremony, but alcoholic beverages are an absolute necessity.

In some areas, where ethnic nationalities reside, people usually make a condolence visit with meat and alcoholic beverages. For example, in Miao Ethnic Nationality villages, when someone passes away, all the families in the same village usually present some jin (a Chinese measure of about half a kilogram) of alcoholic beverages, rice, and other things to the family whose member has just died.Relatives are supposed to offer much more than the villagers. For example, the son-in-law of the family usually presents twenty jin of alcoholic beverages and a pig. Accordingly, the family offers a dinner and alcoholic beverages to host visitors who come to give condolence.

In Nu Ethnic Nationality（怒族）villages in Yunnan Province, when someone passes away, families in the same village usually offer condolence to the afflicted family by bringing them alcoholic beverages. A sorcerer slowly pours alcohol into the mouth of the dead, while all the attendants each drink up a cup of alcohol. Their activity is called "Departure Drinking（離別酒）."

In ancient China, when the dead body was placed in a tomb, people also placed alcoholic beverages in front of the tomb, so that the dead person could continue drinking in the underworld as he did while he was alive.

Notes: 1) primitive 原始的　2) sorcerer 巫師　3) feast 宴會　4) unoccupied 空著的　5) symbol 象徵　6) deceased 死亡的　7) conventional 慣例的　8) token 標誌　9) mourn 哀悼　10) condolence 弔唁　11) departure 起程　12) tomb 墳墓

12 酒德和酒禮 Morality and Etiquette of Drinking Alcohol

The words "jiude"（酒德）first appeared in The Book of Shang（《尚書》）and The Classic of Poetry（《詩經》）. These words imply that alcoholic drinkers should abide by certain moral codes while drinking. In particular, they

should not behave like Zhou, the last king of the Shang Dynasty（商紂王）, who indulged in alcoholic beverages without restraint. The Book of Shang contains a chapter entitled The Document of Prohibition Against Alcoholic Drinking（《酒誥》）that represents Confucian teaching on the morality of alcoholic drinking. It says that alcoholic drinking is not permitted except on occasions when a ceremony is held to worship deities. In addition, people should not gather together to drink alcohol. However, Confucian morality does not prohibit alcoholic drinking. It instead allows people to use alcoholic beverages to honor supernatural beings, show respect for aged family members, and entertain guests.

If someone neglected this etiquette in a social setting, drinking excessively and exhibiting reckless behaviour, senior participants would express disappointment at his/her conduct.

Yuan Hongdao（袁宏道）of the Ming Dynasty observed that many drinkers failed to observe drinking etiquette. He thus wrote an essay entitled The Policy of Alcoholic Drinking（《觴政》）. Although he wrote the essay specifically for those who conducted the proceedings of alcoholic drinking in a social setting, his essay suggests general guidelines that common drinkers can use to adjust their drinking according to the accepted standards of behaviour.

In ancient China, people often followed the following drinking etiquette.

When hosts and guests drank together, they would kneel down face to face and touch the ground with their foreheads. It was the way to respect each other.When junior and senior members drank together, the juniors would first of all kneel down and kowtow, and then they would be seated in order of their positions. The juniors couldn't drink the wine before the elders.They had to wait until the elders completed their alcohol.

Usually there are four steps in the ancient drinking etiquette.

（1）A host and a guest perform a courtesy gesture by kneeling down face to

用英文了解中國

face.

(2) The host pours a bit of alcohol down to the ground in appreciation of the kindness of Earth for providing grains and foods.

(3) The guest sips alcohol and expresses his/her appreciation of it to the host.

(4) At last, both the host and guest take up their cups and drink the alcohol.

At a banquet or dinner party, a host usually raises his glass to guests for toasts, and the guests will respond accordingly. Both the host and guests exchange short complimentary speeches when they toast one another. Usually the host and guests stand up from their seats while toasting one another. These toasts may involve only two people or everyone at the table. The guests may toast among themselves.

Notes: 1) classic 古典著作 2) imply 暗示 3) abide by 遵守 4) indulge 沉迷於 5) morality 倫理；品行 6) Confucianism 儒教 7) supernatural 超自然的；鬼、神的 8) etiquette 禮儀 9) excessively 過分地 10) reckless 輕率的 11) conduct 行為 12) specifically 特別地 13) proceeding 程序 14) guideline 指南 15) kneel down跪下 16) complimentary 稱讚的

13 酒與道教 Alcohol and Daoism

Daoism or Taoism is China's native religion and originated with its Han Chinese ethnic majority. Long before Daoism arrived on the scene, alcoholic beverages had been used in a variety of magical activities. In addition, alcoholic beverages were used as sacrificial offerings for supernatural beings and blessings for humans.

Influenced by this ancient tradition, Daoism in its early stage generally did not prohibit alcoholic beverages. The Five-Dou-of-Rice Sect（五斗米教）, an early Daoist sect, had its own religious discipline that fell into three sections, each having three items. But none of these items concern the prohibition against drinking

alcohol.

In the early Jin Dynasty, Wang Chongyang（王重陽）founded a new Daoist sect called the Quanzhen Sect（全真派）. Qiu Chuji（丘處機）, a disciple of Wang Chongyang, issued a system of precepts for all Quanzhen priests to follow. Near the end of the Ming Dynasty, Wang Changyue（王常月）founded the Quan-zhen Conglin Sect（全真叢林）. Its canon included the Three Major Sections of Precepts（三堂大戒）containing hundreds of items, one of which prohibits drinking alcohol.

Some Daoist scriptures even contain rules to penalize Daoist priests who violate even one of these precepts. Strictly speaking, Daoism does not restrict ordinary Daoist believers from drinking alcohol, but it does strongly oppose alcohol abuse because it can lead to heedlessness.

One of the Daoist scriptures gives the following details of harmfulness related to alcoholic beverages.

(1) Alcohol making wastes grain.

(2) Alcohol drinking causes damage to health.

(3) Alcohol drinking interrupts daily schedules.

(4) Alcohol drinking endangers the stability of a family.

(5) Alcohol drinking negatively affects the commu-nity and the vitality balance of Heaven and Earth.

The same scripture even stipulates stiffer penalties such as flogging with a whip or reducing the status of those who abuse alcoholic beverages.

Notes: 1) originate 來自於 2) influence 影響 3) sect 教派 4) disciple 弟子
5) precept 戒律 6) canon 教規 7) scripture 經文 8) violate 違犯 9) harmfulness
危害性 10) interrupt 中斷 11) stability 穩定 12) negatively 消極地 13) penalty

14 酒與佛教 Alcohol and Buddhism

Buddhist precepts prohibit both Buddhist laymen and monks from drinking alcoholic beverages. Buddhist Mahayana and Hinayana stipulate their followers to refrain from drinking alcohol. The Agama Sutra（《阿含經》）includes the following five precepts.

(1) Avoid killing or harming any living being.

(2) Avoid stealing. Do not take what is not yours.

(3) Avoid sexual indulgence.

(4) Avoid lying or any hurtful speech.

(5) Avoid alcohol and drugs, which diminish clar-ity of consciousness.

Buddhist laymen and monks abide by many additional precepts relating to lifestyle and social behaviour. However, the act of taking the five precepts constitutes one's formal entry into Buddhism and represents a serious religious commitment to Buddhism.

Some Buddhist scriptures or sutras issue the following list detailing the harmfulness of alcoholic indulgence to people in the secular world.

(1) Alcoholic indulgence causes the loss of wealth.

(2) Alcoholic indulgence causes damage to health.

(3) Alcoholic indulgence causes quarrels and fights.

(4) Alcoholic indulgence ruins personal reputation in community.

(5) Alcoholic indulgence brings out a short-tempered rage.

(6) Alcoholic indulgence blunts the senses.

Buddhist precepts do not merely forbid people to drink alcoholic beverages themselves, but they also prohibit them from encouraging others to drink and be engaged in any alcoholic business.

Buddhist precepts related to alcoholic drinking are designed to help Buddhist followers extinguish any secular desire along the Eight-Fold Path（八正道）in order to attain Nirvana, a condition beyond the limits of the mind, feelings, thoughts and ecstasy.

Notes: 1) Buddhist 佛教的　2) laymen（別於僧侶）俗人　3) indulgence 放縱 4) hurtful 有害的　5) diminish 減少　6) clarity 清楚；明晰　7) consciousness 意識　8) commitment 承諾　9) secular 世俗的　10) quarrel 爭吵　11) short-tempered 急脾氣的　12) rage 狂怒　13) blunt 鈍的；不鋒利的　14) extinguish 熄滅　15) ecstasy 狂喜

用英文了解中國：

五千年歷史精華，美食美酒、奇葩典故，外國人怎麼能不懂！

編　　著：楊天慶，楊磊

發 行 人：黃振庭

出 版 者：崧燁文化事業有限公司

發 行 者：崧燁文化事業有限公司

E - m a i l：sonbookservice@gmail.com

粉 絲 頁：https://www.facebook.com/
　　　　　sonbookss/

網　　址：https://sonbook.net/

地　　址：台北市中正區重慶南路一段六十一號八
　　　　　樓 815 室

Rm. 815, 8F., No.61, Sec. 1, Chongqing S. Rd.,
Zhongzheng Dist., Taipei City 100, Taiwan

電　　話：(02)2370-3310

傳　　真：(02)2388-1990

印　　刷：京峯彩色印刷有限公司（京峰數位）

律師顧問：廣華律師事務所 張珮琦律師

定　　價：250 元

發行日期：2022 年 09 月修訂一版

◎本書以 POD 印製

國家圖書館出版品預行編目資料

用英文了解中國：五千年歷史精華，
美食美酒、奇葩典故，外國人怎麼
能不懂！ / 楊天慶，楊磊編著 . --
修訂一版 . -- 臺北市：崧燁文化事
業有限公司 , 2022.09
　　面；　公分
POD 版
ISBN 978-626-332-737-5(平裝)
1.CST: 英語 2.CST: 讀本 3.CST: 中
國文化
805.18　　111014075

電子書購買

臉書